# A Pocket Full of Memories

## Jean Ann Williams

# Reviews

This lovely story picks up with the Monteiro family after Claire and her siblings have grown and made lives for themselves, despite the fallout from their mother's struggles with mental illness when they were children. Dotty waits for her children to come home for Mother's Day but is sad to know that one child, Lolly, will probably ignore the invitation. Lolly still hasn't gotten over the rejection she felt after her younger brother, Chipper, was born and her mother mysteriously disappeared from her life as Dotty sank into the black haze of depression that commonly follows birth. It's been two years since the family has heard from her.

I can't think of a better Mother's Day gift than to have your children come home and fill your life with love and forgiveness. Even though the visit lasted one day, it's clear the emotions will carry Dotty through the rest of her life. Such an uplifting book can't be missed.

Angela Moody, Author – No Safe Haven (2016); The Belle of Oyster Bay (2020).

This story made me tear up and gave me goose bumps! I love the back to basics and wholesomeness of the characters best of all! The story reminds me of the importance of family and especially the bond between a mother and daughter. The book is hard to put down and I enjoyed it immensely. I'd recommend it to everyone.

Crystal Martinho Hatter, Correctional Counselor

# Dedication

I dedicate this book to my mother,

Carol Jean Robinson,

and my mother-in-law, Wanda June Williams.

Both have been constructive and encouraging examples

for my life as a Christian mother.

# Acknowledgements

To my husband Jim, thank you, dear heart, for loving me these fifty-two years. Thank you also for being the techy guy who keeps my computer running.

It takes many people to publish a book. First I'd like to thank my Lord God for giving me a creative imagination. His strength living in me keeps me going no matter the obstacles in life.

Thank you to the first readers: Crystal Hatter and Angela Moody.

A huge thank you to the other team people who have made this book a reality: Editor Barbara Oden, for her edits, ideas, and manuscript assessment to make this grow from short story to novella length; editor Lee Carver, for teaching me more about Deep POV, her expertise with the editing process, and the creative process in tips and wise words for preparing a book and its cover for publication. Thank you to Arielle Shaina for the exceptionally magnificent illustrated cover. And thank you to the cover designer, Louis Edwards, for making the cover shine.

# 1

Dotty Monteiro rose early Saturday morning with plans to bake a strawberry pie. At her vanity table, she brushed massaging strokes over her scalp and through her salt and pepper waist-length hair. Thoughts of her five children sent a shudder through her aching heart. Dotty slumped before her mirror. She and her husband Pete would spend another Mother's Day alone.

After coiling her hair into a soft knot and securing it with two hair combs, she entered the kitchen. She slipped a brand new rose-patterned apron over her head. It had been a gift from her eldest child, Claire. She'd sent it to her for no special reason. Just because, which was so like her. Dotty pressed her palms over the skirt of the apron. Time to give the goats their hay.

Bare feet stuffed into rubber boots, she walked to the large barn used for goat hay, supplies, and farm implements to keep their acreage orderly and producing. As she wrestled apart a thick slice of alfalfa, she thought of the years of work they'd done. She and Pete had left the San Joaquin Valley of California because her doctor said her constant lung problems were due to the bad valley air. And worst of all, from the crop dusting on their cotton and corn farm.

When they saw the advertisement for this ninety-nine-acre property, Pete drove the five hundred miles to see the place and buy it, while Dotty stayed back and packed. In a few years, their California farm would go to an older brother, which left Pete and Dotty free to move anywhere they chose.

Even though Pete didn't buy it sight unseen, Dotty did, and she was once again glad for her smart husband and his choice for their dream home. A sign had greeted her when she arrived at the new home: Shaver Christmas Tree Farm. Dotty had ceremoniously taken down the sign after they purchased the place. It took them years of work to make the farm perfect for them.

Now, standing on the step of the barn, she took in the view of the twenty acre pad of usable land. There stood the log house, a creek many yards behind their home and out of sight, and in the back of outbuildings and animal pens, the meadow. To her right, the overgrown Christmas trees were a forest. This spot was a grazing area for their growing and healthy goats. Dotty sighed in her contentment. Her small herd chewed off the fir tree leaves they could reach bite by bite and left a nice shady area underneath for the hot days of summer.

She glanced at the old logging road behind the outbuildings and to the left of the grazing area for the goats. The road climbed their mountain and spread out to include the rest of the ninety-nine acres where her young children had explored. They bought the land before Chipper was born. It was the only home their youngest had ever known. It didn't matter that he was born and lived for a few short months in the wilderness of Northern California.

At the goat pen, Dotty flipped the latch open on the wooden door of the feeding window. The three does stuck their heads out, already taking bites of hay as she divided their breakfast between the two racks. "Good morning, you hungry ladies." She chuckled and scratched their itchy hornless knobs when her hands were empty of their alfalfa.

The younger goat, Glow, blinked and chewed. Dotty smiled. "Yeah, Miss Glow, I'm a little early today." Glow cupped her back in a stretch, her pregnant belly lowering toward the ground.

The older, dominant goat, Jasmine, kept jerking bites and nodding her head as she ate. Dotty patted her soft black and white head. "That's my girl. Eat hearty and give me a half gallon this afternoon. I need the milk to make cheese next week." The youngest doe, Anise, stuck her head between the bars of the rack, making *mmm* sounds as she fed. This fall, Anise would be mature enough at almost two years old to make a trip to the breeders. Dotty smiled. She'd have three milking does next spring. She'd have enough milk for not only cheese and butter, but to make rose and lavender soaps to sell at the farmer's market in the nearest city.

An hour later, Dotty slid a pie into the oven. As she washed her hands at the sink, Pete's bigger and stronger hands slipped around her waist. "Good morning, Mrs. Monteiro." Pete kissed the few soft wrinkles on her neck, wrinkles which hadn't been there two handfuls of years ago.

She leaned against her beloved. "Same to you, Mr. Monteiro. Did you sleep well?"

He mumbled in her hair. "Sure did." He stepped aside and grabbed the pitcher of orange juice from the refrigerator.

Dotty poured herself a second cup of hot peach tea. "Good. I did too." Her lips knotted into a pout. "But I'm fighting sad feelings about missing our children."

Pete didn't answer, sipping his juice with a smile forming on his mouth. "Think of it this way." He wiped his mouth with the back of his hand. "They are independent and doing well. They don't ask for handouts, and they help people."

Tears filled Dotty's eyes. "I know, honey, and I'm grateful. I simply miss them. I haven't celebrated Mother's Day with our five wanderers in three years."

Pete's head angled toward his left shoulder. "I'm certain you'll get five cards today and five phone calls tomorrow."

Cracking eggs into a bowl, Dotty sighed. "Of course, unless Lolly is too busy with her friends to think of me on Mother's Day." She *tsked* her tongue on her teeth. "If so, this will make three years in a row I hear nothing from her on such an important day."

Drawing closer to Dotty, Pete tucked her into his arms and spoke near her ear. "I'd still like to tell her how she hurts you, but that would be the wrong way to go about it." At that Dotty shook her head against his collarbone. "Then, when are you going to sit Lolly down and explain how she hurts you? Scripture teaches when you've been hurt to go to that person and tell them."

Dotty took a backward step. "You know how she can be, Pete. Everything, no matter if it's true or not, is my fault." She squinted at him. "If I brought up the lack of contacting me on Mother's Day, she'd be hurt I made her out as though she were thoughtless. And truly, so many of her problems are because of me."

Pete grabbed her in a fierce hug. "Yes, but it was not your fault. Chipper's birth was harrowing. You didn't make it so after having four children, it just was." He kissed her deeply, and she pressed into him, wrapping her hands around his neck. Could she ever help Lolly understand? Possibly she wouldn't until she had her own children, and maybe not even then.

Fixing their breakfast of scrambled eggs and whole-wheat biscuits, she silently prayed, *I want to learn to have a grateful heart for our independent and wonderful children who love You, Lord. Please protect Lolly and let her feel my love.* Dotty pulled apart chunks of biscuit dough and dropped them in a cast iron skillet. She slid the biscuits in next to the pie. *Thank You for hearing my prayers for Lolly. I continue to pray that one day we'll become friends and not just mother*

*and daughter and what feels sadly like enemies to me.*
*In Jesus' holy name, I'm grateful. Amen.*

Dotty set the table and retrieved two empty, sculptured glasses from the freezer. She poured goat's milk into each one. As an afterthought, she plunked down Pete's favorite: a pint jar of elderberry jelly. She looked at the burl clock with their family picture on its face. The mail would come in an hour, and she couldn't wait to receive cards from her children. Drawings of hearts and X's and O's would not be in these Mother's Day cards from grown children. Dotty had a file full of cards signed that way. She'd saved each one so she could read them again and satisfy her hungry heart.

As she pulled the biscuits from the oven, she thought of her three grandchildren. She hadn't seen them in almost a year. Weary feelings overwhelmed her. She whispered, "What happened to my prayer moments ago from my supposed-to-be grateful heart?"

Independent children were indeed a good thing. It's just—well, their independence sometimes chafed hard on a mother.

# 2

Dotty had another counter to wipe clean when the postal truck pulled alongside the Monteiros' mail box stand. "Oh, good." She dropped her dish cloth, ran the lung-pumping jaunt on the graveled driveway, and opened the metal door of the mail box. Her hand searched inside and withdrew the white and pastel colored envelopes. She jogged back to the house and sat on the porch bench. "I'm going to savor each one, opening them in between chores."

Dotty sorted through the envelopes and placed them in birth order, but—not one from Lolly. Fanning the envelopes like playing cards, Dotty shuttered her eyes to block the tears. At age twenty, Lolly still had not forgiven her.

Pete let the screen door bang shut as he came outside. "Got the cards, I see."

She blinked. "Except for Lolly."

They walked back into the kitchen together. "Give her time, Dotty. Her card may just be late."

Dotty's neck stiffened. "I'm unsure how to reach our Lolly, Pete. I'm wrong if I do and wrong if I don't."

He stood by the sink with her. "She's the baby girl of the family." Pete's lips curled toward his graying mustache. "Everyone did everything for her, especially after Chipper." He shrugged. "Claire took over as mother for so long. Maybe that's why." He hugged her. "That's all it is, I'm sure." Releasing her, he moved to the front door. "I've got to fill the porch with wood. With these cold mornings and nights, we'll need fires at least another few weeks." Her husband let the screen door bang shut.

Dotty finished tidying the kitchen as the aroma of warm strawberries permeated the house. Stooping before the opened oven door, Dotty lifted the glass pie dish and sat the bubbly dessert on a wire rack. She stood back and admired her lattice crust with red juices staining the edges. "Eating this pie will cheer me."

She reclined in a chair to rest her back and sip an iced mango green tea. "Hmmm, just what I needed. Thank You, Lord, for good drinks."

Sensing rejuvenation, she pulled an envelope from one of her apron pockets. She examined Claire's envelope with the way she looped the first and last letters in her name. She chuckled at something their ClaireLee said when she was only thirteen. She placed hands on hips and begged her dad, "I like just Claire, Daddy. I'm not a baby anymore, so don't call me ClaireLee."

Dotty shook her head at the idea two names together were for babies. It took a while, but she and

Pete honored her request, although they would slip a time or two and call her ClaireLee.

She studied Claire's return address. Cottonwood, California was less than three hundred miles from Dotty and Pete. It sounded so far, but Claire lived the closest of their five children. Time to read her eldest child's card. On the front of the card there were roses of various shades of purple. Claire knew her favorite flower and colors.

Inside, white space, except Claire's handwritten note:

*Dear Mama,*

*I pray that Mother's Day is restful and filled with the love of your children.*

*Do you remember the very first quilt we made together? That, Mama, is one of the best memories I have with you. I finally understand your patience in teaching me to sew. I'm making quilts with Roxy. I love you with my whole heart. God bless you, Mama.* It was signed, *Claire, Donald, Roxy, Adam, and Baby Tara.*

Dotty's tears drip-dropped on the words, startling her, because she hadn't realized they were so near.

She swiped the wet from her cheeks. The quilt. Ah, yes, she did remember, and it seemed like yesterday . . .

\*\*\*

"Mama, I'm home." Eleven-year-old Claire's boots thumped on the oak floor. "Where are you, Mom?"

Mama raised her head from deep inside her clothes closet. She hollered over a shoulder, "In my bedroom, honey."

Claire stood behind her mother, resting a hand on her shoulder. "Mama, guess what I want us to do?" Claire then jumped as though startled. "Daddy. What are you doing in there?"

Pete stood on a short ladder to the right of the extra large closet and was bringing down a medium-sized box. He descended the ladder. "Helping your mom get the heavier boxes."

Mama squatted, sitting on the back of her heels. Dust tickled her face. "I give up. What do you want to do, Claire?" She rubbed her nose with the back of a hand.

Claire came around to face her mother and squatted. "Make a quilt."

Mama rotated into a sitting position, crossing her legs at the ankles. "Really? You finally want to sew?" She'd hounded Claire to sew with her from age eight, but she complained it was too hard.

Pete set the box on the floor nearby. "Good for you, Pumpkin. Your mom is the best teacher around." He grinned at both of them.

"Thanks, Daddy." Claire smiled and joined her mother on the floor. "I sure do want to sew. Rachael and her mom finished a quilt they made with their old clothes. She showed it to me today and it's sooo, sooo neat. Please, can we make one?"

Mama wiped another shoe with her rag and nestled it back in the closet. "May we, Claire, may we, and we sure will."

Claire clapped her hands. "Oh, yea. Do you want me to go through the rag drawer?"

She stood. "Yes, and pick out the less worn clothes for the quilt."

Her daughter jumped up, ready to begin. "And if I need to, I could also ask each person in our family if they want to donate a piece of their clothing they'd like to see in the quilt. Thanks, Mama, it'll be so fun." And off she ran, only to return when she'd gotten halfway across the room. "At the top of the quilt, I want to sew in gold letters JESUS IS LOVE. I just know it will be beautiful. May we do that?"

Mama reached for her daughter's hand. "We sure will, sweetheart." She glanced at Pete. He walked toward his dresser and opened a drawer.

Claire raised her hands in the air and hurried from the room. Her yell echoed from the hall. "Whoopee!"

Mama stuffed herself into the pit of the closet, and then twisted and sat on the floor. Pete stood before her, holding a green T-shirt. "Our girl is growing up, Dotty."

"Yes." She smiled and nodded her chin at what Pete had in his hands. "What's that?"

He shook it out and displayed it. "My favorite tee."

"Oh, Babe." She looked closer at the holes and paint marks. "Are you giving that to—?"

"Look, Mama, these were in the rag drawer." Claire came back with an armload of clothes. She dropped the pile next to Mama and sat beside her. She held up a T-shirt. "This doesn't fit Lolly anymore, and it's clear of stains on the sleeves. See?" She stretched out both sleeves, an abundance of yellows and reds, as though wanting her to inspect them.

Mama drew closer. "Well, you've got a good eye in the basics for creating quilt pieces, honey. Yes. Let's use this." She pointed. "See what your daddy has?"

Blinking, Claire's eyes grew as round as acorns. "Is that for the quilt, Daddy?"

He nodded and handed the tee to her. "My contribution, sweetheart." He ruffled her hair and left the bedroom in an easy stroll. His long legs in motion made Dotty's heart yearn. Yearn for his embraces and kisses when it was just them alone.

Claire dropped the shirt on her left side as though making a keep pile. "And how about this?" She raised a blouse in the air and beamed a smile at her mama.

Bending for a closer look, she took the blouse in her hands. She turned it this way and that. "Why is this with the rags?" She raised her chin to seek Claire's face.

Head bowed, Claire muttered. "It wasn't in the rag drawer, actually."

"Oh?" She angled her head to study her daughter's expression.

Peeking at her, Claire's lips quivered. "I'm sorry, Mama. I slipped the blouse in because I have no clothes in the rag drawer."

She dropped the blouse and hugged Claire to her. "It's okay, honey, but I think we can find a more worn piece of clothing from your closet. Don't you think?"

Claire nodded. "You'll help me, then?"

"Of course." She rose from her sitting position and arm in arm, they went into Claire's room to sort through the clothes to find the perfect piece of clothing for the quilt.

*** 

Now, sipping her tea, Dotty tried to remember. How long ago was it that Claire asked to make the quilt? She counted nineteen years and remembered they had entered it in the county fair. It had won second place. After that, it became Claire's quilt on the bed she and Lolly shared. And to think of what happened two years later. With Dotty and Chipper's almost death. The birthing had been hard. Harder than any baby she'd had before.

Dotty shook her head. Easing herself from the chair, her back felt strong and rested. She needed to iron their clothes. Afterward, she'd read the next child's card.

Dotty halted her steps at the guest room doorway where her ironing board came into view. Pete walked in with a handful of brown and white eggs. He'd also carried a bit of the chicken pen ground beneath his boots. Dotty wagged her head and *tsked* her tongue, "My, my, you're giving me more work."

He bowed his head, seeming to stare at the black on the carpet. "I'll clean that." His eyes met hers, and his twinkled like a mischievous boy.

"Good, and thank you, Mr. Monteiro." She grinned. "I was going to iron a few clothes. But"—she tilted her head—"how about I read Liam's card to you first?"

Pete grinned. "I'd like that." He raised the eggs higher. "Let me put these away first and clean up the mess on the carpet."

Dotty seated herself in the rose-patterned loveseat in her favorite corner of the room. When Pete returned, he settled next to her. Reaching into her pocket, she removed the envelope from their second child, slipped a fingernail under the seal, and lifted the card for them to view.

# 3

Decorated with scenic mountains and a waterfall, the bright greens and blues of Liam's card made it splash with color.

She read aloud, "'May your Mother's Day be filled with love and joy, and may the Lord bless you throughout the rest of the year, Mother, and always.' He signed the card, 'We mean what the card says, Mom. We will be contacting you. We miss you and love you, Liam and Veronica.'"

Together, she and Pete studied the artwork on the front of the card. Dotty sniffled. "Remember how much Liam loved mountains with the hunting, fishing, and hiking?" She arched her neck to peer at her husband's face, to check his expression. He grinned. "Liam got that from me, didn't he, Pete?" Pete's eyes shimmered like glass and Dotty sighed. She saw God in His creation of the flora and the fauna.

Dotty patted his hand. "I'll never forget when I drove Liam to the mountains for this first buck hunt."

His eyes shifted toward the window overlooking the chicken and goat pens. "He was twelve years old. Why was it that you took him?"

Her lips lifted with the pleasure. "Remember Liam asked you to take him buck hunting, but you had the job waiting in Washington State?"

Bowing his head, Pete's voice grew soft. "I felt like a heel for not taking my own son on his first hunt."

"Oh, no, sweetheart." She slipped her fingers through his calloused ones. "This is a memory I'll always cherish."

Pete's eyes brightened. "Well, then, I guess it turned out all right. I liked it that Liam could still go with you. But, Dotty, I missed too many of our children's events."

"Someone had to work, Pete." Dotty fiddled with the heart on a chain around her neck. "Besides, we both are aware it took years for me to physically and mentally be stronger after Chipper's birth. I really appreciated your decision to help Neecy Wolf move all the way from Gallagher Springs to come live with us, so she could help take care of our family. Once I had recovered I was glad you agreed it was best that I continue as a stay-at-home-mom."

He brought her hand to his lips and kissed it. "Yes."

"And about hunting with Liam, you made time to hunt with him later."

"I did." His eyes sparkled.

She chuckled. "What a great idea for you and Liam to go bear hunting when you finished building the house in Washington."

Leaning closer, Pete's breath caressed her ear with his whisper, "I know you enjoyed taking Liam hunting for his first time."

Dotty snuggled into his shoulder as Pete cuddled her with his arm. Yes, Liam's excitement made her even more eager to take their trip. After long goodbyes and promises to bring back surprises she found in the woods, like rocks, pinecones, an exotic bird feather and such, she settled the other children in with their neighbor, Norma.

She glanced at Pete. "You remember Norma, right?"

"How could I forget?" He grinned. "She had a habit of celebrating everything from Ground Hog's Day with a picnic lunch on her deck, rain or shine, to having a pizza night once a week. We were always invited."

"She treated us like family. And I'll never forget her kindnesses. Like how she took care of the rest of the kids the day I took Liam on his deer hunt."

Memories in living color wafted over Dotty's mind. About an hour after she and Liam left his siblings at Norma's, they'd parked in the mountains and hiked across the rim and down one of the hard-to-reach canyons. At her favorite hour to scout, they walked like hunters, they took three steps, stopped to listen, three more, stopped again. Finding a hidden spot to view a stream, they sat to watch and see if deer would come for water.

Five hours later, as the sun touched the mountain range, she and Liam took the route to the top hoping to see a buck on the climb. After a hard climb they arrived seventy yards from the top, where a distinct noise to their right halted their steps.

Beyond a dense stand of fir trees, there was a sound like a shuffling of hooves scattering dried leaves within a confined area. She'd whispered to Liam, "If this is what I think it is, that buck's getting wound up."

Liam gave her the thumbs up, and his eyes were as round as a pie dish. They waited for several minutes while the dance of the buck kicked in even stronger. He snorted through his nostrils, a sure sign he courted a doe. Liam pulled his rifle sling off his shoulder and held the gun in his hands. He took quiet hunter steps and continued the pattern until he disappeared inside the trees.

His shot sliced through the forest, and a flock of quail scattered in the brush yards from where she waited. After a minute, she ventured into the trees. When she came into view of Liam, he was gazing in her direction. He jutted his chin to point downhill. She came closer, and he spoke. "I got him." They walked on, following the buck's blood trail down the mountain. Soon enough, she spotted him lying on his side next to a stump. She and Liam counted the curved antlers, three on each side of his head.

"Mom," Liam gave her a lopsided grin, "I've brought down meat for the family."

Her own chest had puffed with pride. "Looks like you did, Son. I'm proud of you." She hugged him in congratulations.

Then her smart son pointed. "We'll wait half an hour to make sure he's no longer alive, so he won't jump up and stick us with those massive horns. Right, Mom?"

She agreed. "You're always thinking ahead."

After half an hour, Liam waved her forward. "Let's go, Mom."

As they stood over the deer, she pointed at it. "Son, do you want to thank God for the gift of food?"

In response, Liam bowed his head. "Dear God, thanks for this buck. He died so we may feed our bodies. In Jesus' name. Amen."

They lifted their heads, slapped palms together, and began the work of bringing out Liam's buck.

It took them almost three hours to dress him out and pull him the rest of the way up the mountain where Liam shot him. They had tied the deer with Liam's rope and threw the other end over a tree branch farther uphill. Then they hoisted the deer as far as that tree, slipped the rope off that branch, and chose another one a little higher up and repeated the pull. It was exhausting, but they couldn't have dragged the deer uphill any other way. That was the longest fifty yards of her life. After helping to lift the carcass and tossing it into the Bronco, her arms and legs wobbled like cooked noodles. "Son, I'm not as strong as I used to be."

He pounded her back. "Thanks, Mom. Not everybody's mother loves to go hunting more than shopping."

She chuckled. "Give me the woods, instead, and a sweet son to boot any day."

After they had hung the deer from the rafters of the garage to cure a day, Liam headed for the house. "I'm calling Dad."

She hurried behind him and got Pete's number for Liam. After Liam waited a few seconds, he yelled in the phone, "You won't believe it, Dad. I shot a three point at around 3:30. My first day hunting."

She sat in the kitchen chair with a glass of sweet iced tea. As the cold liquid raced down her throat and revived her, she listened to Liam tell their hunting story. She didn't want to repeat what Liam had said, so she added in her mind what Liam left out so she would tell Pete her side of the hunting story later.

\*\*\*

Pete stirred from their quiet moment together during which she'd pondered the old hunting story. He stood up, stretched his large frame, and indulged in a yawn. Dotty's reverie broken, she stood also and took both their tea glasses. "Pete, you certainly made it up to Liam the next year when the two of you went hunting."

Pete grinned. "Liam bagged a trophy buck." He pantomimed Dotty taking a photo. "I love that picture you snapped of me on one side of the deer holding a horn and Liam on the other side holding the other horn."

Dotty and Pete walked arm in arm into the hallway. She could still recall the excitement on both their faces when her finger pressed the button on the camera.

\*\*\*

When Pete left to work outside, Dotty got busy ironing. And when she hung the last pressed garment on a hanger, she glanced at her watch. Time to start lunch.

She set chicken thighs to soak in a pan of fresh goat milk and placed two potatoes in the oven to bake. Bending to retrieve a baking dish, her apron dangled in front with the weight of two more cards left to read in the pocket: from her youngest sons, Grayson and Chipper. She thought of Lolly and the ache from missing her card.

Keeping her hands busy in the preparation of the meal, Dotty worked hard to remember past the fuzzy months after Chipper's birth. Way back to a point in time that may have changed Lolly. Of her four children, Lolly was least excited over Dotty's pregnancy. How did that go? What did Lolly do? Or say—?

She would have to go back to Chipper's beginning.

After she was about to miss her third cycle. After her queasy tummy would not go away. And after the first flutter moved within her womb, she had no more doubts. She would have another child, and deep in her heart, she was excited. The baby was not planned. She and Pete felt four children were manageable. To their way of thinking, they could give equal attention to their children. Two boys and two girls. Perfect-sized family.

They understood this was not for everyone, the smaller family, but it's what they felt was best for her. She'd had a miscarriage in between her live births. They were too hard on her, causing havoc on hormones and her broken heart. It took months before she pulled through the valley of depression and felt healthy once again. She hated that she had a bout with depression. For whatever reason, so had her grandmother.

She and Pete thought they'd been careful those almost three years.

Not careful enough.

She sent Pete a letter to where he was working the tunnel and told him. And she reassured him this baby seemed strong, with her having no cramping. Claire was older and would be a big help. If only God would help her believe those reassurances. She had no idea someone else would have a hard time with the news.

When she could no longer hide her mound of baby belly and when she grew certain she had indeed passed the danger stage of losing her baby, she sat her children down in their spacious living room. Four pairs of eyes watched her. Sure everyone would be happy, she smiled. "I have news. A huge, wonderful surprise."

Three-year-old Lolly's shoulders perked upward, her eyes round. "What, Mama?" She came forward and leaned on her mama's knees. "Tell me."

She held Lolly's hands and she gazed at Claire, Liam, and Grayson. "You're going to have a baby brother or sister."

Gasping noises met her ears. When she lowered her chin and leveled her eyes on Lolly's expression, Lolly's lips puckered. "No, Mama. No baby."

She jerked back in her chair so sudden, she felt her womb lunge forward just a tad. Surrounded by the other children giving her hugs and kisses on the cheek, one of them said in her ear, *"Yippee."*

Claire said, "I want a sister."

She looked down at Lolly, who wore no joy on her face but a scrunched and knotted scowl.

What was a mother to do?

# 4

Dotty was at a loss then. She was at a loss today. It had been too long to count since she last received a Mother's Day card from Lolly Francis. In elementary school Lolly made her cards, but they were class assignments. From the day Lolly expressed her anger over the birth announcement, she made sure to include Lolly in the preparations for the new baby. Together, they washed, dried, and folded the diapers. She showed Lolly the baby clothes the newborn would wear. Lolly wrapped herself in the baby quilt that had been hers when she was a baby. And Lolly acted excited, if not more than a little possessive over the quilt.

But the birth did not go well. Lolly fell through the cracks created in the family by her near death and long-term recovery. Without a mother's guidance, Lolly was taken care of by her siblings. Pete told her later Claire did most of the nurturing of her siblings as much as she could at only thirteen.

Sometimes, Dotty knew she could do nothing to solve Lolly's problem. That it was up to Lolly to work out her issues of the past when she was no longer the baby of the family. But there was always guilt. A mother's guilt. For a time, she could no longer be the mother her children needed. The loss of blood after Chipper's birth left her weakened. To this day, her memory lapses made it impossible to recall whole weeks. She couldn't help feeling ashamed. Shouldn't she have been stronger? But, no. The doctor said her hormones and her loss of blood put her body out of whack. This could disturb the mind. Especially her history of having a sensitive nature, something her mother said she inherited from her mother's mother.

Yes, Lolly was spoiled until Chipper. Dotty tsked her tongue. Pete was right. It was no one's fault. It just happened.

She added parchment paper to the baking dish, making cleanup after eating the chicken thighs easier. Something they could afford easy enough. Oh, how she could have used the extra funds they had now to make kitchen work a cinch back when she was raising her children. She had parchment paper, a dishwasher, and paper plates, though the dishwasher was used to sterilize the jars for her goat milk.

How does the mother of a wayward child turn off the worry of regret? She'd learned not to let it gush like a waterfall, but it still trickled like a stream. Someone once said, "Turn your concerns into prayers." Dotty tsked her tongue again. She needed to practice those wise words quicker and more often. That was for sure.

Lolly had given Dotty half of her gray hairs, and she herself gave the other half. Too much in the way of regrets after Chipper's birth.

Raising her face to get serious with God, Dotty squeezed her eyes shut. "Lord, whoever said grown children are much easier on the heart has never had them."

After a satisfying lunch with Pete, Dotty placed her hands on her full stomach. "I overate. Our new garden potatoes are the best, don't you think?"

"You bet." The ice in Pete's glass chinked as he took a long drink of sweet tea. He rose from the table. "As usual, you're harvesting a great garden, Dotty." He kissed her with a smack on her mouth. "I really love your beefsteak tomatoes." He winked. "If you need me, I'll be out by the chicken pen leveling the ground before I build our new turkey pen."

"Glad you enjoyed the tomatoes." She gathered a few dirty dishes to carry to the sink. "When will the baby turkeys arrive?"

"Within two weeks."

She was unable to continue the conversation as the bang of the screen door announced his departure. One side of her mouth lifted in a grin. She loved her man. Always building. Always busy creating something from wood. And he always wanted her to see his progress, because she was generous with the *ohhs* and *ahhs* over his work.

Isn't that what wives were supposed to do? Build their men up? Making them feel appreciated and making them realize how special they were?

With Dotty it came easy as she truly respected and honored her man. He had stood by her after Chipper's birth during the hollowed-out months, and she'd stand by him today.

Having cleaned her kitchen of pots, pans, and dishes, Dotty sat on the front porch swing and pulled Grayson's card from its resting place in her apron pocket. She would read his card first and then put on her sneakers to take her afternoon walk. Before she tore the envelope, she studied his address. Grayson loved Greenland, where he was a missionary to the natives. The overextended mother on the front of the card made Dotty laugh out loud. She had on an apron and carried a frying pan in one hand, a broom in the other, and a child sat before her with a thermometer in his mouth. Dotty read: *Mothers are supposed to cook, clean and take care of you when you're sick.* She opened the card. The cartoon characters continued, with the mother and son in a small car, traveling through European countries. *You are an award-winning mother, because you also spent time with me when I was a kid.* Grayson then wrote, *I love you, Mom! I pray your day satisfies the desires of your heart.* He signed it, *God bless you, love forever, Grayson.*

She stared at the card with the names of famous cities around the world. Even though it had been a dream of Grayson's to travel, and he did, it was something they never did together.

Dotty slipped on her tennis shoes and took the steps off the front porch. Hurrying in her fast walk, she marveled about how her exercise regime had changed as she had aged. She thought back to the time she was in their garage with her thirteen-year-old son, where he had a few weights and bar bells. And him teaching his mama how to pump iron.

***

Grayson made a fist and pumped his arms in the air. "C'mon, Mom, don't you want to get into shape?"

"Not like that." She pointed at the bulging muscle on his upper arm. "And not with those." She tapped one of the cast iron weights on the bench bar. "I have no desire to have manly muscles, Son." She patted her thighs. "Just need to get rid of this fat. I can't seem to do that since Chipper's birth six years ago."

Grayson threw back his head in laughter. "No, Mom, you should do light weight workouts at the bench. Much lighter barbells too. Honest, it'll get rid of it and make you strong!"

She moved toward the door of the garage-turned-gym. "No, thank you."

"You're not getting any younger." Grayson sang the words. "It's now or never." He play-wrestled with her, mussing her hair. "Ah, little Mama, please?" He raised his brows as though a brilliant idea struck. "We'll even work out together."

Waving him off with her hand, she grimaced. "Okay. Besides, I'd love to spend more time with you."

He grinned. "I'll plan your workout schedule and write it down. Then I'll show you how it's done." He gathered pen and paper from a small shelf. "You can go, Mom. I'll get this to you when I'm finished."

She crossed her arms, tucking fists under them. "I better not get hurt."

He raised his face from his notebook and studied her. "I'll take good care of you, Mom."

She, in turn, ruffled Grayson's brown mop of curls. "I plan to take this weightlifting thing slow, young man."

As the days became weeks, Grayson coached her until her routine became perfect. In the months following, she never hurt herself, and was pleased no manly, bulging muscles showed themselves. If she flexed her biceps at Grayson's request, two nice goose eggs, as Grayson called them, rose on the top of her arms. Her body firmed and shed pounds. The best part? She and Grayson trained at the same time. She appreciated him more for his generous nature and his way of making her feel special.

***

A happy and contented sigh spilled from Dotty's lips as she made a u-turn to walk back home. She was in better health because of Grayson. Dotty had become a jogger along with Grayson's regimen and got up to five miles a day, six days a week.

Yes, she owed Grayson her admiration and her complete trust. Dotty could honestly say Grayson had never had a bad attitude toward her, where the other children, when they were teens, had sassed a time or two. Lolly a whole lot more. Not so with Grayson.

When she and Grayson talked on the phone they still encouraged each other to eat healthy and get plenty of exercise. She walked even faster. *Lord, I haven't seen Grayson in two years. And I know he's spreading the gospel and doing Your work. Would You bring him home to visit? If it's Your perfect will. In Jesus' name, I ask. Amen.*

# 5

After her walks, Dotty's back always felt stronger. With renewed energy, she entered the kitchen, washed her hands, and gathered sterilized jars from the dishwasher. She'd need those to milk into.

As though Jasmine could tell the time, she bellowed. Dotty settled the milking supplies in a clothes basket she used for this purpose. "Mercy's sakes, that goat can tell when it's four o'clock."

Pete tiptoed from behind, acting sneaky, but she could sense his presence. Then he wrapped his arms around her waist. "Are you talking to yourself again, my love?"

His happy mood and the sweet terms of endearment came more often than usual for one day. She inwardly shrugged and leaned against his chest. She'd soak him in and feel his peace. "Yes. Why not? It's too quiet in this house with no children and one loud goat that sounds more like a jet scream."

"What does Jasmine want?"

Dotty faced him. "Her grain. Of course." She moved away from Pete and gathered the paper towels she almost forgot. She squinted at her husband. "It's been too long since Grayson's last phone call. Don't you think?"

He walked to the refrigerator freezer with an empty drinking glass. "For Mother's Day, you'll be hearing from each of the kids."

Dotty's prayers had made her hopeful. "Maybe even Lolly?"

Pete opened the freezer door and dropped ice cubes in the glass. He filled it with sweet tea. Lifting the glass, he said, "To our children, whatever they may be doing." He waggled his brows.

She stared at him, watching him closely. He must be trying to cheer her up because tomorrow was Mother's Day, and they'd lack time with their children. "We had fun with them when they were small, didn't we?" Dotty made an effort to be cheery with him.

He swallowed the tea, and when it was empty, the cubes clinked in the glass. "Yes, we did. Even when it was difficult, I played with them and read to them in the evenings when we moved back from Gallagher Springs to our home here. Having more time, I knew I could help Claire while you recovered from Chipper's birth."

She understood his meaning about it being difficult and lowered her eyes. "That was a harsh time in our family. I think, Pete, this is Lolly's main problem. I became an absent mother after she'd been so spoiled for three years previous to Chipper's birth and my convalescence. God was good, though. The baby and I didn't die."

Pete hugged her. "Yes, sweetheart, you and Chipper lived. I'm grateful." The catch in his voice did not escape Dotty's notice, and her jumbled emotions stirred within her heart.

Both of them jumped at Jasmine's jet scream screech. "Big mouthed goat." With a slight grin, Dotty hurried to the task at hand. "Some days I threaten to myself that I should sell her."

Her husband said over his shoulder as he headed outside ahead of Dotty and held open the door, "No, you won't. Who would want an old, noisy goat? Besides, she's like one of your own children."

After Pete went in one direction and Dotty walked toward the goat pen, she couldn't help but recall the night she delivered Chipper in a cabin in the wilds of Northern California. So many times before and after Chipper's birth, she regretted Pete taking the highway tunnel job. But it was planned. After Pete left, she discovered she was pregnant, which was a great surprise. And he had already settled into the tunnel job.

To make matters worse, she fretted because it was dangerous work. He blasted rock through a mountain to make a better road for the growing traffic as people flocked to the Northern California area. But the hard reality was they were about to lose their land and home. This home. So because work was scarce, Pete had to leave for a planned year and blast rock. That way they could make the tax payments on their Oregon home. But fear gripped her when she discovered another little one stirred beneath her heart.

She told him in a letter. And even though her
parents were nearby, Pete came home two weeks before
the expected due date. It was a weekend, and he packed
up his family and took them back with him to live in the
wilderness.

Her labor came within hours after they got to the
cabin. Hard and fast. No time to rush to the hospital
fifty miles away. She hemorrhaged during and after
Chipper was born in the cabin. They arrived at the
hospital as she and the baby were near death. They
spent several weeks in the hospital where she received
good care and regained some of her strength, if not her
nerves. God brought them through.

Out in the milk barn, Dotty settled on the milk
stool and relaxed her shoulders. She also recalled how
devastated she became when days turned into a week
and more away from her other children while in the
hospital. Pete kept reassuring her Claire took care of
them. But her own nerves frayed a bit each day as she
imagined her needy Lolly without her care. She often
wondered, would Claire know how to calm Lolly when
she cried for her mother? Would Claire see to it Lolly
still got the attention she needed being the youngest
until now?

What would Claire do about them starting school?
As far as she could remember, Pete never said, although
with her mind scrambled, it took all she had to heal
physically and nurse her new baby. In between the hard
work of recovery and nursing, she fretted that this

separation from her children and Lolly would put a wedge between them.

Sure enough, later on after months being back in the cabin, Lolly still shied from her. Claire was her mother. And how Lolly felt about Chipper? She could not remember, but she suspected from how Lolly was distant with Chipper later on, she had become jealous of the new baby who was always in the bedroom with Dotty. She remembered that much. Rest. She had had to rest way too long behind the closed bedroom door.

Now as Dotty milked her goat, her hand pushed upward and squeezed. The milk pinged into the glass jar in a steady cadence. Today, her normal prayer time was focused on Lolly. Because of her, Dotty owned Jasmine who turned ten years old last month. She still gave sweet, rich milk with cream at its thickest in the spring. It rose two inches or more thick in a quart jar.

Dotty recalled Lolly's friend had a mother goat with twin doelings. Lolly had insisted Dotty go with her next door to see—

\*\*\*

She scraped off a spoonful of cinnamon-spiced cookie dough with another spoon and onto a pan. It took a long time for life to return to somewhat normal. One from which it seemed impossible to get them back on a normal track. Especially Lolly. She thought of this when she woke this morning, which became the reason for Lolly's favorite cookies about to go into the oven.

She hoped Lolly would see her mother's love through the cookies.

The screen door banged, making her drop the spoons.

Lolly yelled, "Mom, Mom."

"I'm in the kitchen, Pumpkin, making cookies."

Ten-year-old Lolly breathed in gasps, perhaps from a long run. She peered over the cookie baking pan and gushed. "Snicker doodles, yea." She opened and closed the utensil drawer. "May I have some dough, please, please?"

She dropped another teaspoonful of dough in the last spot on the cookie sheet. "Only one spoonful, Lolly." She frowned. "I see you've chosen a tablespoon. Only one for sure with a big spoon." Slipping the cookies into the oven, she straightened her knees and shut the door. "Where have you been, honey?" She giggled at the dirt on Lolly's face as she touched the tip of her freckled button nose.

Lolly dug in with her spoon, licked it clean, and chewed. After yum, yum, yumming, she smacked her lips. "That's what I came to tell you. I've been at Ashley's holding a newborn baby goat." She squealed. "Oh, Mama, you have to come see them. There are two, and, and"—she blinked—"I want one." She dumped the empty spoon in the sink with a clatter.

She stood from a bent position after cleaning a spot of flour off the floor. She planted hands on her hips and scowled. "You want a what?"

"Goat." Lolly folded her hands as if in prayer. "Oh, please, Mommy, please. They're white and cute, and they're called Kinder goats." She pointed a finger at her mom. "Remember, you just said the other day you thought we needed to get some goat milk. You said goat milk is the best, much better than cow milk. You said Chipper would do better on goat milk because of his allergies. Remember?"

Oh, dear.

Her jaw slackened and her mouth gaped open. How many times had Lolly used Chipper to get what she wanted? He needed this toy or that toy which she played with also. He needed new socks which she had caught Lolly wearing a time or two. It didn't matter they were boy socks. She shook her head. Was Lolly really thinking of Chipper this time because of his rashes from cow dairy? Or? Or herself? "Yes, indeed. I said that, but Chipper hasn't even tried goat milk. I've been waiting for Norma's goat to deliver, and then Chipper would try it. I'm not buying a goat from Norma and Ashley only to find it doesn't help him."

Lolly gripped her hands together again. "Okay, Mom, you have to come see the babies. Norma says she'll have extra milk to drink when the little goats are two weeks old. Chipper could try it then just like you planned."

She huffed. "Lolly Francis, you just don't quit, do you?" She spread her arms wide. "I'm in the middle of baking. You can wait until I'm done." She whirled round and began washing the soaking dishes. The

familiar squeeze in her chest from irritation made her
purse her lips. Honestly, the child tried her patience
time and again. Here she was making her favorite
cookies and she wanted a goat. Stubborn to the bone.

Lolly wrapped her little arms around her mother's
waist. "Thanks, Mom, I'll help rinse."

Well. Okay, then. That smoothed her hackles and
melted her heart.

Four months later, the Monteiros bought the
Kinder doeling twins and took them home. They settled
the doelings in the new goat barn and pen area Pete had
built, and Lolly learned to care for them. Almost two
years later, when the time came, they sat with their
grown does when they each gave birth. With much
impatience from everyone in anticipation, the
Monteiros enjoyed goat milk. Chipper thrived on the
milk.

Lolly seemed to take pride in helping her baby
brother get rid of his rashes. Maybe the rough patches
with Lolly were behind them. She could only hope.

# 6

Shaking off the memories, Dotty squeezed the last drops of milk into the jar. She reached upward and patted Jasmine's bony hip. "We've been doing this a long while, haven't we, ol' girl?" Jasmine craned her neck and blinked her doe eyes at Dotty. Moments later, the goat responded with a healthy belch.

Leading Jasmine back to the barn, Dotty thought of the remaining card. Should she wait until after supper or should she read Chipper's card before? She checked her watch: almost five. It would have to wait. Pete met her on the porch steps. "Don't make dinner tonight." He took the basket of supplies and milk from her and entered the house.

She followed a few steps behind him. "But why?"

Pete sat the basket on the tiny table in the kitchen. "I want to take you out to dinner." He waggled his brows.

"Oh." She grinned. "How nice. No dishes tonight."

He grabbed her hand. "I do want you to sit on the porch with me and read me your next card." He left her side. "I'll get two sweet teas and you put the milk away."

"Sounds perfect." She began her chore while humming "Amazing Grace."

Pete and Dotty moved around the kitchen. She strained the milk, and he gathered two tall glasses. She pressed the timer for thirty minutes and set the two quarts of milk in the freezer to cool faster to enhance the flavor. Ice cubes clinked in the glasses followed by the pouring of tea.

Leaving the kitchen, they both settled on the porch bench. "Would you like to see the two cards you didn't read first? And I'll read the last one aloud to you."

Sipping on his tea, Pete reached for the cards. "Thanks, Babe." He read each one and when finished, Dotty dug into her apron pocket and took out the final card. Chipper's return address was as it had been for years. As a captain on a fishing boat, he had a P.O. Box in Sitka, Alaska. She opened the envelope.

She read out loud, "'Happy Mother's Day to the best Mother a guy could want.'" It showed three cartoon characters, each dressed in appropriate uniforms and playing baseball, football, and basketball.

Dotty pointed. "Just like Chipper." She turned to the inside. It showed a mother in a housedress with a bandana on her head, holding pom poms for each of the sports. "'Mom, you are the greatest fan a son could have. God bless you. I love and miss you. Chipper.'"

Dotty grinned. "Oh, how that boy can touch *my* heart." She wiped at her eyes. "Is it because he's the youngest or because he could have died before he took his first breath?"

Pete stared straight ahead as if pondering the question. "Both."

She blew her nose on a tissue. "Just what I thought, also." She wadded the tissue and stuffed it into the now-empty apron pocket. Dotty gazed at the card again and chuckled. "I'll never forget when Chipper entered college."

He touched her shoulder. "And I'll never forget how you planted yourself in the middle of his football life."

"Well, Pete, what is a mother to do when your eighteen-year-old son calls you and tells you he's ranked third in the state?"

She most certainly would not forget.

\*\*\*

As the phone rang, she hurried to answer before it went to the answering machine. "Hello?"

"Mom, I have good news, and I have bad news."

"Hi, Chipper," she began to rub her forehead, the beginnings of a headache, "tell me the good news first."

Chipper's voice rose higher. "I just found out I'm third in the state in both passing yards and touchdowns, and first in the state in interceptions."

She choked on her next words, "Oh, my stars."

Chipper cleared his throat. "May I read you a line from the college newspaper?"

She lay down a pencil on the grocery list she was preparing. "I'm listening, Son."

"The article is titled, 'Monteiro Works the Playing Field,' and here's the best part, Mom. My coach says, 'Chipper Monteiro may not be the perfect player—this work horse acknowledges he's made mistakes. But Monteiro has also made enough excellent plays to override the mistakes. He's one who gets the ball out fast to other players; it's on time and precise. He spreads the ball around.'" Chipper paused, and then said, "Mom, I'm glad I decided to attend college instead of taking the railroad job in Portland."

"I'm glad for you, Chipper Frank. You're getting this football itch out of your system, and you'll have no regrets or 'what if's' to look back on."

Then he gave her the bad news. "We're about to lose half our guys because some of the freshmen are not getting up and going to their morning classes. If they get kicked out of classes, they are kicked off the team."

"Why are they sleeping in?"

"Probably going to parties until late at night, I guess."

"That's just plain wrong." she blew an exasperated breath. "Everybody on the team suffers."

Chipper lowered his voice. "Tell me about it. I don't know how we'll manage without back-ups, Mom."

She took a sip of her cooling hot tea. "I plan on being at your game tomorrow."

"Will Dad be there?"

"I'm afraid he'll be working, Son. You understand he'd be there if he could." After she hung up, she finished the grocery list and dove into the task of making Chipper's favorite fudge with chopped walnuts. When Lolly came in from classes at the local college, Dotty made the announcement. "I'm going to Chipper's game tomorrow."

Lolly held a quart of Jasmine's milk in her hand. "You are?"

She nodded, and Lolly launched into how she was always there for Chipper. How she always babied him. She poured the cooked fudge in the buttered dish, ignoring her daughter's sassy mouth. "If you can come, that would be great. If not, I'll be okay to drive the short hour by myself. I have to show support for Chipper and his team. You know how hard it is on Chipper that your dad misses his games. And it's hard on your dad not being there."

Lolly poured the milk into a glass, her eyes blinking as though making a decision. "I will not cancel my plans with my friends." She shoved the quart of milk back into the refrigerator and slammed the door. "So, you can just go alone." Lolly stormed from the room.

Would the jealousy never end? At that moment she didn't like her own daughter. Her next emotion filled her with guilt. Shouldn't parents not only love their children but like them as well? Tears stung. She knew without a doubt she would always regret how she felt about Lolly on this day.

The next day, once she arrived at the football parking lot of College of the Dunes, she ate a tuna sandwich in the car. Afterward, she headed to the bleachers. The game went in the Dune's favor with a lead of 27-14. But the other team capitalized on the Dune's mistakes, and took the game with a score of 30-27. Chipper played a tough game, but there were fewer relief players than usual to give team members a rest.

She watched for Chipper to leave the locker room. When he emerged, a broad-shouldered man met him at the entrance. Chipper nodded and appeared to listen to the man. She walked over and stood next to them and waited.

The big man slapped Chipper on the back with a meaty hand. "You played a good game, Monteiro, but we'll be losing more team members before next game. Those freshmen are putting us at risk for the last two games."

She figured he was Chipper's coach, so she interjected, "I could solve your problems, Coach."

Since she was standing behind him, he turned to face her, eyes squinting. "And you are?"

She extended a hand to shake his. "I'm Chipper's mother, Dotty Monteiro. I'd pound on every freshmen door and get those boys up and to class on time." She nodded for emphasis.

He accepted the shake. "I'm Ben Holloway. You're serious about getting the freshmen up in the mornings? Would you do that the full week and a half?"

She puckered her lips and wrinkled her nose. "You better believe it, Coach Holloway."

The coach scratched his head. "I give you permission to knock on every freshman team member's dorm door for the next eight class days. This just may work with two more games left. Follow me, and I'll get you the names and whereabouts of each freshman's room."

With Pete gone up north on another job, she had made a sudden decision and took matters into her own hands. When he found out, he wasn't surprised, considering the circumstances.

The next day, she knocked on doors and double-checked to make sure every boy headed to class. With the tougher sleepy heads, she had a statement memorized. "Okay, you lazy boy, you better open this door. What would your folks think if they knew you were flunking college? You better hope I don't call them and give the sad report."

The plan worked, and of course she had to sweeten the deal. Every morning, she gave each freshman a piece of Chipper's favorite fudge as they walked out of their dorm room on their way to class. The freshmen stayed on the team with the Dunes going on to finish the season strong, winning their last two games.

\*\*\*

Pete stood and stretched. "I can't remember if I told you, Dot, but I prayed every morning as you traveled the winding road to and from Chipper's college. Getting those kids to assume their responsibility to the team saved the season."

So he did remember. Sometimes she wondered if he even knew what went on in their family when he was somewhere else working. Dotty wiggled her brows. "It sure didn't hurt to give them a slice of fudge. And everyone is clueless to this day that I use goat milk cream to make fudge."

Bringing in the empty glasses from their front porch, Dotty's eyes met his smiling ones. "Thank you, sweetheart. That was a fun adventure, and as far as I know, I never made one boy angry. They were as polite and respectful to me as I could have hoped." She ran hot water over the glasses to rinse them. An unexpected ache twisted around her heart. Tears pricked her lashes, and she bowed her head, and sobbed. "I just can't stop thinking . . ." she paused to let the catch in her throat pass ". . . about, about how Lolly was so angry."

Pete wrapped his arms around Dotty, her head tucked under his chin. Dotty worked to gain control of her weeping. "She was so adamant that I cared more about Chipper." She raised her face to his. "You understand it's not true, Pete. Right?"

"Yes, yes." He cradled her tighter. "Of course, sweetie."

She sniffled. "I'm so lost. I want my daughter back."

And with his soothing murmurs, the flood of tears gushed until Dotty grew weak and limp. Pete steadied her, half walking, half lifting her to the kitchen chair. "Rest a bit, Babe. And just let me say this." He knelt in front of her. "We raised them to become independent, and that's a good thing." His voice changed to one of deep emotion. "Let's not talk about this anymore, or I'm going to bawl too."

She soft-punched his shoulder, grateful he moved them away from the topic. "But you're my man of steel."

He kissed her full on the mouth, sudden and quick. "Don't flatter me." His eyes simmered, showing his need of her. "Or I'll have to pack you on my shoulder and fly us to the moon."

She sighed. "I'll be okay."

"Good." He kissed her again, and this kiss was strong, long, and yet soft. Dotty melted into his kisses. She forgot for a moment about wayward daughters and unfulfilled Mother's Days of years past.

# 7

After Pete left through the front door, Dotty blew her nose and headed to their bedroom. He said he'd like to leave for dinner in fifteen minutes. She approached her closet and chose a coral dress with a pattern of tiny, white shells. When she slipped it over her head, it came down to her calves and covered her knobby knees. Brushing her long hair, she held it at the base of her head to prepare a ponytail. Dotty vowed to concentrate on the current moment. Dining out sounded delightful.

As she washed her face, her phone on the nightstand rang. Dotty shut off the faucet and dried her face. She grabbed the receiver before she lost contact.

"Dotty?"

"Yes, Marti."

Her breath came in rasps as though she ran a marathon. "Dotty, are you expecting company?"

She chuckled. "No. What makes you ask?"

"Well, you see, I was halfway to my mailbox, when low and behold, four cars passed my driveway headed your way."

Dotty's chest heaved. "I wonder who it could be."

Marti sighed. "That's why I called. I thought surely you'd know if you were having company." After a few seconds, Marti added, "And then I wondered why I wasn't invited if you were having a Tupperware party or something."

"Of course I'd invite you if I had planned a get-together. I'll tell Pete, and we'll go out to meet whoever it is. Thanks, Marti." After she rushed out the door, she slipped into her sandals.

***

Dotty waved her arms at Pete. He had pulled the tractor under its covering as he did every night if he had used it that day. He jumped to the ground. After she told him the news, he took Dotty's arm and steered her toward the front of the house. But not before a tiny grin wiggled at the corner of his lips. "Let's see what's going on."

Dotty blinked.

Holding hands, they stopped on the lawn as a car maneuvered into their driveway. She glanced at her husband. Grinning down at her, his eyes softened.

"Pete?" She swallowed, and a tremor grew over her whole body.

He slipped his arm to her shoulder and whispered, "Happy Mother's day, Mama Monteiro."

As his arm held her close, Dotty recognized two of the cars and her hands flew to her mouth. She suspected moments ago by the grin on Pete's face, but she didn't dare to hope. A cry of joy escaped from her lips. "Really, Pete?" She jumped up and down as she faced him and squealed.

Tears glimmered in his eyes. "Yes, really."

The cars stopped and pulled Dotty's attention toward them. Doors opened and family piled out. Running, with arms outstretched, was her eldest granddaughter, eight-year-old Roxy. Trailing behind Roxy were her siblings Adam, five, and Tara, almost two years old. Pete and Dotty's children and their two in-law children, Donald and Veronica, sauntered behind the little ones. After Dotty and Pete hugged their grandbabies, they stared at their children standing there with smiles as wide as the love Dotty held in her heart for them.

She studied each face while they said, "Happy Mother's Day." She let go of the grandchildren and rushed to her fully grown babies' arms.

Claire's eyes glimmered with tears as mother and daughter kissed. Liam gave his mother a first rate bear hug. Chipper and Grayson took turns swinging their mom in their arms as though she were a child. Grayson, whom Dotty hadn't seen in two years, said in a husky voice, "Hey, little Mama, we're home."

Everyone embraced in a group hug with laughter, tears, and the guys slapping one another's backs.

Claire's and Liam's spouses came closer. They waved, and even at a few yards away, Dotty could tell they were misty-eyed. "Get over here and give your mother-in-law a big hug." They did, and she planted kisses on their cheeks.

After visiting in the yard, people dragged their suitcases out of their cars, and Dotty's shoulders sagged. Where was Lolly? Did she truly care so little about her own mother? Dotty didn't want to ruin the moment, but she needed to ask. Then again, did she really want to hear another excuse and possibly see the pain in her other children's faces? In her mind, she shook her head no. She would keep quiet. But maybe she could take Pete aside soon and see if he knew if Lolly was yet to arrive.

Inside the living room, Dotty's face had grown warm from excitement. Pete sat cross-legged on the carpet in a corner, with grandchildren huddled near him and on his lap. She had to say it. "Mr. Monteiro, you knew about this."

With his chin bobbing, his grin wobbled. "I kept the secret really well, didn't I?"

She puckered her lips and relaxed them as she faced her children. "You should have heard me whining and fussing earlier today. I complained about how I missed you and wondered out loud to your father if I was going to see you all together again."

Pete placed Adam higher on his lap. "I bit my cheek more than once to keep a straight face. At one point, I wished I knew nothing about the surprise. It got harder by the hour," he waved his arms across the room, taking in their family, "to keep this from you."

Chipper leaned against a wall with his hands in his jean pockets. "Yeah, Dad, we could always count on you no matter what."

Pete's smile faded. "Even when my job took me away from home more than any of us wanted?"

Grayson raised his chin. "Even then, Pops." He walked to where his dad sat and kissed him on top of his thinning hair. "That's for all you've done for our family."

Pete's eyes misted. "Well, I couldn't have done it without your mom and Claire's ability to run things. To keep everyone going in the right direction."

Dotty's face grew red hot at the compliment. "We couldn't have done it without God's love and strength. I learned to call on His name sooner rather than later when I needed His guidance. When I was feeling overwhelmed because I couldn't be a better mom all those lost years."

"We've planned a party, Mom." Grayson stood near the sofa and faced his mother. "This party begins today and goes into tomorrow on Mother's Day." He folded his hands. "Before that, though, let's each of us say a prayer of thanks in honor of you."

Each child took turns saying a few words of gratitude for not only their mother, but their father also.

With bowed head, Dotty's tears of gratitude dripped between the fingers of her folded hands. It took every bit of her emotional strength to keep from sobbing. When the prayer ended, she said her own silent prayer for her wayward daughter, wherever she may be.

# 8

Dotty sat in the recliner at her children's request to watch as they brought in bags of food and decorations in honor of the Mother's Day party. Her heart simmered with love, while her children laughed and busied their hands turning the dining room into a party scene. All for her. Her jaw slacked at one point when Chipper brought in a large sheet cake. Claire was behind him with a glass punch bowl filled with glass cups. Dotty had a sneaky suspicion Claire would make Dotty's favorite punch with lime ice cream and clear soda pop.

Her three grandchildren ran around decorating the walls with balloons their daddy helped them blow up and tie. Should she be concerned about the masking tape on her painted walls? She shook her head. *Be grateful no matter* came to her right then. Grateful? How about ecstatic? Awed? Tongue-tied? Dotty sighed, more rested in heart than she'd been in years. Then the nagging thought came to destroy her joy.

What about Lolly? Dotty's wayward baby girl?

She shoved it far from her and placed the thought at Jesus' feet. Wasn't the Lord the very reason she became filled with awe? Only God would orchestrate such a thing as this.

When the decorations were placed around the dining room, which included the block letters "Happy Mother's Day" strung across the picture window, Dotty's children ushered her to her chair at the head of the table.

Claire clapped and everyone hushed. "Mom, my children made you a gift. And they want to place it on your head."

Roxy, Adam, and Tara carried a paper crown on a platter, holding it together as they walked to Dotty's chair. Each of their faces shining with glee, with a shy smile here, a brow high in anticipation there. All three grinned. Dotty gasped at the crown's beauty. She clasped her hands to her chest.

Roxy spoke first as they placed the platter on the table. "I cut out the crown and cut the top to make spikes." The crown itself was gold-colored, making her feel like a queen.

"It's so beautiful, honey." Dotty touched it with the tip of her finger.

Adam leaned closer to Dotty. "I glued on the beads." He pointed. "See, Nana? The beads spell "Mother of the Year."' He lifted his eyes toward Claire, and she nodded.

His shy smile brought fresh tears beneath Dotty's lashes.

Little Tara pushed between Roxy and Adam, "Nana, Nana, I color." She stabbed a chubby finger,

"Here. Here. Here," at the purples, reds, and green marks made with a crayon that covered the crown. Tara fisted her hands together at her chin and grinned at her nana. "It so pretty, huh, Nana."

Dotty was grateful for Tara's jabbering. She worked hard to gulp back the sobs which grew within her achy throat. Pushing back her chair, she grabbed all three grandchildren in a hug. She swallowed. "I—love your art work. You've made Nana feel very, very special today." Over the tops of their curly brown heads, she focused on Pete. He sat at the other end of the table, his eyes moist with tears.

After the grandchildren placed the crown upon her head, Claire's husband said, "Hey, everyone. I have an announcement." The room grew quiet. Donald stood on the outer edges of the dining room with his hands behind his back. "Claire, why don't you sit down next to your mom?"

Her brows rose as she sat in a chair on Dotty's right side. Claire blinked at her husband, a hesitant smile on her lips. Donald took side steps and kept one hand behind his back. "I have two things I want to say." He settled near Claire and watched her as he said, "We're going to have baby number four around Christmas time."

The room exploded with cheer, handshakes, back slaps and hugs. Five minutes later, the room calmed. Donald wiggled a finger to their children. "Okay, kiddos, time to surprise Mommy."

All three of Dotty's grandchildren moved as one to their mother's side. But not before Roxy grabbed something from her daddy. At a nod from Roxy to her siblings, they all sang, "Happy Mother's Day, Mommy."

Claire gasped, hands covering her mouth. Roxy stood on her tiptoes and placed a crown on her mother's head. She kissed her mother's cheek and stepped back. "We love you, Mommy."

Adam started forward, but Tara beat him to it. "Mommy, Mommy, you's a queen too."

Claire opened her arms and folded them into her arms. "Thank you, sweet peas. I love my crown."

After a few more minutes of bragging over her children, Claire, along with Dotty, accepted their plates heaped with food: a bean dip, guacamole and sour cream, tortilla chips, and chicken tamales that Claire and her family had made. The tamales were melt-in-your-mouth delicious. The best Dotty had ever tasted. Being a person who paid attention to details, she couldn't help notice some of the tamales on people's plates had only a little filling and were thick with the corn masa. She had to ask. "Claire, you and your family know how to make tamales. And it's such a job, I imagine the children helped." Her forehead scrunched with her question.

"Oh, yes." Claire took another bite, chewed, and swallowed. "Even Tara made a few tamales until she got bored." She chuckled. "It was a family affair."

Dotty wiped her lips with a napkin. "Did you freeze some?"

She nodded. "Making tamales is so time consuming, we made plenty and froze about half of what we brought."

Chipper gave a soft burp. "Can I come to your house on the next tamale day meal?"

Claire nearly choked. She cleared her throat and smiled. "Yeah, sure. All you have to do is sail your boat on over to the closest dock to us and drive the rest of the way."

"Well, I just might do that." He leaned back in his chair. "I do have time off from the fishing industry."

The guys jumped on that topic, drilling Chipper about what it was like to own his own boat and do commercial fishing in Alaskan waters. Everyone agreed that Alaskan fish tasted the best.

Right then, Dotty said a silent prayer. She needed the Lord to continue to keep her baby boy safe in stormy weather.

After the meal, Liam's wife Veronica served a chocolate sheet cake with white frosting and one coral-colored rose on top for Dotty and Claire. Dotty was not surprised by her favorite punch, the fancy glass cup filled with soda and lime ice-cream floating on top.

Halfway through her slice of cake, Dotty could eat no more. Claire wrapped it with a napkin to save it. Although, Dotty asked for seconds on the punch, and Chipper filled her cup. Wanting to sit back and watch her happy family and to hear about their homes and all they did in a day, she settled into the recliner once again. A spot of punch dried on the lap of her spring dress. She didn't need to talk. Only to listen. She found if she remained silent long enough, they answered most of her questions. Their chitchat between the four of them and their dad told her much.

After she finished her punch, she found her eyelids drooping. Her chin lowered to her chest. When it grew quiet, she startled from her dozing. Pete stood over her. "You're not used to staying up late. Is it your bedtime?"

Dotty rubbed her eyes. "Not before I help settle everyone into their rooms."

*** 

It took an hour to get her family situated. One bedroom had dirty sheets, so Claire and Dotty changed those out for fresh ones. This was another of those times Dotty was grateful for a big house with four bedrooms. One room had a double bed, which Claire and Lolly had shared. Another room was the boys', a bunk bed with a trundle. Pete built the trundle when Chipper outgrew sleeping with one of his brothers. The other room had been a toy and playroom turned guest room with a king waterbed which used to be Pete's and hers.

As Dotty's family shut their bedroom doors, she stood in the hallway and stared at her doorway. Why was she no longer sleepy? Pete would be up till late like a hoot owl. Her feet moved toward the kitchen to find him. Sure enough, he had his ice cream bowl in front of him on the counter. Next to him was a half gallon of vanilla ice cream with peanuts and swirled with chocolate. She crossed her arms, his back to her. "I'm not sleepy anymore." She walked to his right side. "I think I'll take some of that."

Pete swiveled to her, his brows raised. "Since when do you eat ice cream this late?" He dug into the yummy delight and scooped up another heap. "You'll get a bellyache."

She reached for her own bowl in the cupboard. "Save me some."

He chuckled. "How much do you want?"

Dotty moved the bowl under his filled ice cream scooper. "One is enough."

They agreed to take their dessert on the porch and sat on their bench, their thighs close enough to feel each other's warmth.

"Yum." Dotty let the creamy delight melt in her mouth. She chewed on a nut. "Honey?"

Pete looked her way. "Yeah?" Another spoonful of ice cream disappeared behind his lips.

"Thank you. You made this Mother's Day the best. It was an answer to my prayers."

He draped his free arm around her shoulders. "Ah, babe."

She elbowed him. "You're not going to elaborate on how you played a part in all this, are you?"

He shook his head no. "This was our children's idea. I just made sure we were home and you were not only hungry, but dressed nice." His grin and the soft, dreamy expression in his eyes made him look boyish. Not the mature man he was now in his early sixties.

Dotty swallowed another creamy bite. "Well, all I can say is—"

Tires on gravel with a noisy engine which cut out pulled near the side of the house.

Pete and Dotty sat very still. It was near midnight. Who could it be?

\*\*\*

Shoes crunched on gravel and came near the porch steps. The porch light became sparse past the steps, so Dotty held her breath hoping, hoping. A shadowy figure came into view and stilled. With her heart-shaped face and wide eyes, Lolly craned her neck and peeked at them. She waved a small bouquet of white carnations at them. "Hi, Mom. Hi, Dad."

Dotty flew past Pete and stood on the lower step where she came to the same height as Lolly. She threw her arms around her daughter and crushed the flowers between them. "You're here. You really came." Dotty wept.

Lolly's arms hugged her mom. "Yes, Mama."

Dotty spoke against Lolly's neck. "I've missed you so much, baby."

Sniffling, Lolly gripped her mama tighter. "I've needed to see you for a long time."

Dotty sensed Pete a few steps behind them. "Hi, sweetheart." His arms enclosed Lolly and Dotty. "We're so glad you came. Is everything okay? You're okay?"

The nodding of Lolly's chin told Dotty it was a yes. Lolly's voice was nearly a whisper. "I've been so homesick. But I've also realized some things. I've ... I've blamed you both for my problems." She was silent a moment, and Dotty stayed quiet and still in Lolly's arms. Was this a confession? Maybe Lolly felt less intimidated to talk if Dotty didn't move.

Lolly sighed like the whole world fell off her shoulders. "I have to tell you something. I ... it's hard to say. To tell you this, but I'm an alcoholic." Dotty froze. Even her breathing halted.

Pete patted Lolly's arm. "Go on. We're listening."

Was there a catch to Pete's voice? Dotty was sure of it. Her own eyes filled to almost spilling, but she blinked against the moisture. This was not about how Dotty felt, but about helping her daughter.

"Well." Lolly cleared her throat, and her fingers tightened on Dotty's back. "I started drinking in college. I hit bottom when I got in a wreck and was arrested for intoxication."

Dotty couldn't help it but she groaned soft and low. Did Lolly hear her? Would it make her shut down and say no more?

"Let's go sit down at the dining room table." Pete moved his hand from Lolly's arm.

"No, Daddy." Lolly lifted her hand. "I don't want the others to hear." Her chin settled on the top of Dotty's head. "This has to stay between us because I'm too ashamed. I'll talk to them when I'm ready. Maybe tomorrow. Besides, I haven't blamed my siblings, only took things out on them. I blamed especially you, Mama."

Right then, Lolly pulled from Dotty. "Mama, before I say the rest, here are your flowers." She handed them to Dotty, and gave her mama a lopsided grin.

Dotty took the flowers and sniffed them. "Thank you, sweetheart."

Lolly cleared her throat a couple of times. "Mama, I blamed you when you couldn't help it. I understand now." Her chin quivered. "I won't lie." She shook her head. "I needed you and you weren't there to mother me. But it was not your fault." Tears streamed along her high cheek bones. "I'm so sorry, Mama. Daddy."

She wiped the tears off her face with the back of her hand. "I went to Christian counseling after being in court." She pointed to her chest. "The counselor helped me to see your neglect of me was not from lack of love." She shook her head, again. "She made me see you were unable to focus. On us. That you had all you could do to care for Chipper and get yourself well. The scripture she had me memorize helped me so very much."

Dotty swiped at two more of Lolly's tears running streaks on her face. "Do you want to share it with us?"

Lolly bowed her head. "Yes, Mama, I do." She sucked in a deep breath and began, "Whatsoever things are true, whatsoever things are honest, whatsoever things are just, whatsoever things are pure, whatsoever things are lovely, whatsoever things are of good report; if there be any virtue, and if there be any praise, think on these things. Philippians 4:8."

When Lolly finished, no one spoke. Dotty clutched at the top of her spring dress. Pete had moved next to Dotty, shoulders touching. She stared at Lolly and was filled with awe. Dotty was about to speak when Pete's body began to shake. A sob burst from him, and he grabbed Lolly into a bear hug, crying.

Dotty couldn't help but throw her arms around them both and cry with him. Their daughter was healed. She'd come home. Lolly cried open, fresh tears along with them. When their sobbing waned, Dotty kissed Lolly and then Pete on the forehead. "I love you both so much." She waited until all their tears ceased. She drew her arm through their elbows. "Come on. Let's go in. I imagine you're hungry, Lolly."

Lolly smiled. "Starved."

Leading them in, Dotty chuckled. "We've got a feast."

After Lolly ate some of the leftover party food and had a slice of cake, she excused herself to get her bags. Once inside, Lolly pulled an envelope from her purse. "Here, Mama."

Dotty's lips curved at the sides of her mouth. "Oh, thank you, honey." She slipped her fingernail underneath the seal and slid out the card. The front had an illustration of a colorful carousel. On top of one horse sat a little girl with Shirley Temple curls. Dotty read the front of the card, "'To the best, the most loving Mother.'" Dotty opened the card, and another carrousel illustration showed a mother and the child on their own horses. Their arms stretched out as though they were soaring. Dotty continued reading, "'We flew through life at the speed of horses. As a grown up, I still want to be by your side through the adventures of life still to come.'"

At the bottom of the card, Lolly had written, *Mama, I'm sorry for all the lost years. Let's make it up to each other. When you need me, I'll be there. All my love, Lolly Frances.*

Before Dotty could speak, Lolly knelt in front of her mother's dining room chair. "Mama." She laid her head on Dotty's lap. "I've missed you more than I can say."

"Honey, honey." Dotty smoothed Lolly's brown hair from the top of her head and down, over and over again. "Sweetheart, look at me." Lolly peered into her mama's face and locked eyes with her. "Lolly, we did lose a lot of years, yes, but you know what I think?"

Lolly blinked. Two tears trailed a path along her cheek bones, and Dotty thumbed them away.

"I think you and I *can* be friends. You're an adult." Dotty searched Lolly's eyes, the chocolate brown surrounding the iris, shimmering. "So let's pretend we've just met as adults." Dotty's smile came soft.

"Let's pretend we don't have a past, if this would be easier." She angled her chin, waiting. Wondering. Would Lolly agree with her idea? Or would she insist on her own way, whatever that may be?

Lolly sniffed. "I'd have to think about it, Mama."

Ah. Dotty expected nothing less from her independent daughter. She held a quickened breath though, hoping she'd know Lolly's decision before she left and went back home to Los Angeles. As a mother, she longed for common ground between them built of stone. Not sand. They needed to move past the confession of guilt.

Patience.

Pete jumped up when the chickens squawked and flapped their wings as though a predator had gotten into their pen. "I'll check on the hens.

Lolly paused. An eternity of a moment. "I do have one friend who was adopted. Her adoptive parents always made sure she knew she was a gift to them. That she made them parents. On my friend's thirteenth birthday, her adoptive parents sat her down and told her she could contact her birth mother. If she wanted to. They would not be offended."

Dotty squeezed Lolly's hands. "Did she?"

Lolly bowed her chin and it came up again in a yes. "It was scary, but she's glad she did. She and her birth mother are now friends. Her adoptive mother is who she trusts to share her secrets and her decisions." She shrugged. "Mama, I want more than a birth mother friendship with you. Could we maybe start there?

Eventually? I hope I can be close enough to you to share my deepest feelings. To be able to ask your advice on life and its trials. But I don't think I could just yet." One side of her mouth lifted in a sad grin. "Of course confessing to you and Daddy was a good start in trusting you again. Right, Mama?"

Dotty leaned closer and kissed Lolly on her freckled forehead. "Yes. A very good start." Something niggled. A question she dared to ask. Should she? Would she cringe at the answer? Dotty tucked a strand of Lolly's hair behind her ear. "I need to know something."

Lolly raised her face again. "Anything, Mama."

The bridge of her nose stung with fresh tears. "Would you share with me who took my place in your heart all these last few years?"

Startled, Lolly's head jerked in her mother's lap. "You won't be angry if I tell?"

"No. I'm hoping, though, it was someone I would approve of."

Settling against her calves and bent knees, Lolly's hands fidgeted on her lap. "Do you remember Norma?"

"Ashley's mom? Whose baby goats you said we simply had to have?" A smile took root and grew within Dotty's heart. It surfaced and bloomed on her face. She nodded, so very pleased indeed. At that second, Dotty could not speak through the knot in her throat. She reached for Lolly and tucked her into her lap once again. "I'm relieved."

Lolly's shoulders heaved with what Dotty knew were fresh tears. As Dotty did when Lolly was a baby with an upset tummy, she rubbed Lolly's spine. Slow and firm. Up and down. Up and down. With a rhythm she hoped would soothe. With a love she longed for Lolly to feel radiating from her palms.

Right then, Pete came back in from checking on the chickens. Dotty and Lolly stood, their intimate moment broken. It was just as well, because Dotty grew spent of emotions. She could tell by the lines in Lolly's young face she, too, had grown exhausted. Although, as Dotty studied her daughter, there appeared a wisp of softness she hadn't seen when Lolly arrived.

Much relieved, Dotty held back the sob forming in her chest. She wanted to allow more room to experience her joy.

Pete shut the door behind him. "When I started toward the hen house, I smelled a skunk. I shined the flashlight, and the tail of a skunk flashed and disappeared under a dug-out spot at the fence."

"Oh, no, Pete. That's nothing but trouble. I hope you can fix that in the morning." Dotty drew her arm around Lolly's waist. "Meanwhile, I should clean the last of the dishes before bed." All three of them sauntered into the kitchen, and Dotty washed the few dishes from Lolly's meal. Lolly rinsed and dried and even remembered where they went in the cupboard. Pete was leaning against the counter near Dotty, when she pointed at him with a soapy finger. "This means you will have to lock the hens in every night. Which means whoever gets up first, and that's me, has to go out there and unlatch the door so they can get out and eat."

Pete was nodding. Lolly squinted. "But, why? I thought they had a large hen house and completely fenced-in yard area?"

Dotty drained the dirty sink water. "No. The old hen house fell down months ago. We bought this portable thing with a hen ladder that includes a bedding and nesting area." Dotty dried her hands. "It was the best we could do at short notice."

After wiping her hands with a dry towel, Lolly picked her teeth with a toothpick. "What do you mean short notice?"

"A year ago, we had a hurricane-like storm." Pete retrieved a clean glass from the cupboard. "It knocked the chicken house down and killed one hen. The rest we found huddled in one corner that was still standing."

Lolly shook her head. "Poor girls. They must have been frightened."

Pete drank the glass of water. "Yep. And it's been several years since we've had any skunks coming around. Or even raccoons." He shrugged. "So we weren't worried about locking the hens in at night."

"Phew!" Lolly pinched her nose. "I think I can smell that skunk."

Dishes done and everyone beyond exhausted, Dotty led Lolly into the guest room with the three single beds. Dotty touched the knob and placed a finger of her other hand to her lips in *shhh*. Lolly nodded. The nightlight Dotty had installed earlier gave off enough light. Dotty pointed to the only empty bed left in the house. Coming farther into the room, Dotty and Lolly stared at Claire's children. Adam was in his own bed. Roxy and Tara shared the other bed.

Dotty whispered into Lolly's ear and pointed again. "This is Adam. He's five. This is the oldest, Roxy. She's eight. And the little one is Tara, two."

Even in the shadows, Dotty could see Lolly's eyes shimmering with tears. "They're so cute, Mama." Lolly grabbed her mom's hand. "One day, and maybe sooner than later, I'll have my own family." Dotty raised one brow. Lolly squeezed her mom's hand. "Tomorrow, I'll tell everyone a bit about what is going on in my life. Hopefully, my siblings will forgive me."

"I'm sure they will, sweetheart." Dotty kissed her cheek. "Sleep well."

"Thanks, Mama." Lolly kissed her mom back. "You, too."

Later, as Dotty readied for bed in her room and Pete showered. Dotty slipped into her sleeveless, collarless night gown. She stopped at her side of the bed near the head and knelt. Bowing her head, she began. "Father, You have given me the gift of my children. They are worth more to me than a mound of gold. Thank You, holy God. Thank You. Please, help me to never forget this time. Help me to earn Lolly's complete trust. Help me to be patient for Your perfect timing when Lolly will trust me. In Jesus' name, I ask. Amen."

When Dotty got her pillow snuggled beneath her head and neck just right, she fell asleep and did not dream.

## 9

Early the next morning, Pete and Dotty sipped their coffee and tea, waiting for everyone to wake. The sun had peeked over the trees in the east only minutes ago, making the front yard of willow trees cloaked in shadows. The two of them kept smiling at each other, and at one point Dotty giggled. She was amazed by what had happened in only a few hours. Pete pursed his lips before a full blown smile bloomed on his face. "It seems unreal, doesn't it, Babe?"

"Yes, sir." She fanned her fingers between his on top of the dining room table. "Surreal. Yesterday afternoon, I was moaning and groaning about missing our children." She wrinkled her brow. "Even cried some." She snapped her fingers. "In a twinkle they appeared."

The sun's glow shone through the tops of drooping leaves of the willow tree. Two doves fluttered from one tree and coo-cooed as they landed on the ground. Necks bobbing, they glanced at Pete and Dotty as though seeing them through the picture window. She had a thought about the doves and was about to share it with

Pete when Grayson bent over Dotty and kissed the top of her head. "Good morning, little Mama." He rustled her hair with a spread of his palm.

Stretching back her neck, she puckered her lips to press a kiss on his cheek. Grayson leaned nearer. She kissed him on his whiskered jaw with a smack. Her boy was a man. "Good morning to you too, Son."

He straightened. "Good morning, Dad." He yawned. "Do you guys get up this early every morning?"

Pete sipped at his coffee. "Sure do. Lots of chores around the farm."

Play slapping Pete's shoulder, Dotty begged to differ. "Don't believe a word of it, Grayson, your dad always gets up about mid-morning."

"Hey, no hitting so early in the morning." He shrugged and grinned. "I'm retired, so why not?"

Grayson's gaze landed on the doves toddling on the lawn. "I miss this place." He rubbed his hands together. "Got any tea, Ma?"

She scooted her chair back. "Sure do. Come on, and you can take your pick." Pouring the hot water into a cup, Dotty handed it to Grayson. "Son—"

Following patter of little feet and a squeal, Adam skidded on the kitchen linoleum in his socks. He came to a halt in front of his nana. He hugged her leg. "Nana, Nana, there's a stranger in the bed in my room." His eyes grew wide in the telling. "I can't see its face."

Grayson bent and gathered him in his arms. "Are you telling a story, little man?"

Adam wagged his head back and forth. "No, sir. Come see." He wiggled as though he wanted down. Grayson shrugged at his mom.

Dotty reached out a hand and stopped them both. "Hold on, guys. I've something to tell you."

Right as Dotty was about to give Grayson the news, Pete walked into the kitchen and crossed his arms. "Your sister has come home."

Grayson scratched behind his ear. "Lolly?" He stared at his parents, his jaw slack.

They nodded.

"Really." Grayson touched Dotty's arm. "This is the best Mother's Day yet, right, Mom?"

"Absolutely. And Son, she wants to talk to all of you later on when everyone is up and around."

"Sounds good to me." Grayson got on one knee and faced Adam. "That stranger in the other bed is your aunty."

Adam cocked one brow in what appeared confusion. "What's an aunty?"

Chuckling, Grayson hugged the little guy. "She is your mom's sister, and you're to call her Aunty Lolly."

"Ohhh." He grinned. "Then, she's our family."

All three adults laughed out loud and in unison said, "Yes."

Tapping his chin, Adam squinted. "Then how come I never met her?"

Pete and Grayson stared at Dotty. As if she had the answers. Dotty held his small hand. "Honey, what's important is today you're going to get to know your aunty Lolly. Won't that be great?"

"Well." He bobbed his chin. "If she's nice to me it would be nice."

Dotty grabbed both his arms and hugged him. "You'll see. She's very nice."

She could only hope Lolly wouldn't leave too soon, but would stay the day.

\*\*\*

In twos and individually, Dotty's children woke. She made a batch of pancakes, and Grayson scrambled eggs. Lolly came in right after everyone else had gotten up. The siblings laughed, the sisters cried, and Lolly became acquainted with Liam's wife, Veronica, and Claire's husband, Donald, and the children.

Once the surprise of seeing Lolly had settled, everyone helped get the rest of breakfast on the table. Lolly made Dotty sit, and Lolly took over pancake making, keeping them warm in the oven.

After a loud breakfast full of laughter and talking over one another, Dotty took Pete aside. "Honey, let's clean the kitchen and give our children time to reacquaint with Lolly." He nodded and loaded one hand full of dishes.

Dotty waded through her family until she was in the middle of the dining room and living room areas. "Your daddy and I are going to clean up. You all visit with one another here in the living room." Dotty wiggled her fingers at Roxy and Adam. "Come children, you can help Nana and Papa."

Claire nodded her thanks. She sat on the sofa, cuddling a sleeping Tara who had her thumb in her mouth. Dotty took over clearing the table, while Pete enlisted Adam and Roxy to help him. She was within ear shot of what Lolly was saying. Dotty kept her head bowed as she worked. Her ears were perked.

"I just wanted to tell you," Lolly said, "how sorry I am that I shut you guys out of my life these past two years."

"We've been *more* than a little concerned," Claire said in her perfect motherly tone. "Especially when you would never take my calls or write me a letter back." She paused. "I thought you were angry at me. That I had done something wrong."

"No, no," Lolly said. "It had nothing to do with any of you. Except, I guess I was pretty angry at the world in general. And … I'd—I had been drinking. I already told Mom and Dad. I was arrested for driving while intoxicated."

Someone gasped. One of the boys cleared his throat. Veronica said, "Oh, no."

"Well." Grayson coughed. "I think any one of us can admit to making poor choices as teens and young adults. Right, Claire?"

Silence.

A sniffle.

Sobbing.

The rustle of shoes as though people moved.

Dotty had to leave the table with another armload of platters. Still, she lingered on the other side of the dining room wall, out of sight and her ears on high alert.

Lolly begged. "Don't cry, Sissy."

Murmured words from Claire, and Dotty leaned closer as Claire said, "…failed you."

"No! You didn't, Claire," Liam hollered. "You did the best you could while Mom was sick." Everything and everyone grew quiet.

Pete's dishwashing halted.

Dotty leaned into the wall.

Even Roxy and Adam stopped talking and stared toward the dining room, wide-eyed.

Except for Claire's muffled sobs.

Liam raised his voice even louder, "Right, you guys?"

"Yep." Grayson.

"Of course." Lolly whined.

The only one who hadn't spoken as far as Dotty could tell was Chipper. She left her spot at the wall and placed the platters on the counter so Pete could wash them. His hands were still in the sudsy dishwater. He frowned at her, started to speak, his mouth open. She tapped a finger at her lips. "It's okay, honey." Dotty moved to the table again to wipe it clean of crumbs and spillage.

Tears pricked her heart as well as her eyes as she made several trips from sink to table.

"It's just, everything was so hard." Claire continued. "I didn't know anything about being a mama when Mama couldn't be one." She blew her nose. "So … so, when Lolly tells us she was arrested, of course I feel it's my fault. I let her down." She blew her nose again.

As Dotty wiped at the last crumb, Chipper piped up in a clear and happy voice. "I turned out real well, so you weren't a complete flop as substitute mom."

Dead silence.

Until.

Grayson chuckled. Lolly giggled. The whole room bloomed with laughter. This was when Dotty had to feast her eyes upon her children.

Each of them either stood, bent, or knelt next to Claire where she sat on the sofa next to her husband Donald. And touching with pat-pats on the shoulder. A rub on her arm. Lolly laid her head in Claire's lap as she'd done with Dotty.

Dotty nodded her head. Her children would be okay.

***

By noon, Dotty and Pete's children had played several games of cards at the dining room table. As a walk down memory lane, they played all the childhood games they missed: Go Fish. War. Memory. And during their card games they spoke of times past, while

Dotty watched and listened from her recliner chair in the living room.

Grayson shuffled the cards for another game of War. "Do you guys remember the pond in Gallagher Springs?"

"Oh, yeah." Liam scratched the back of his head. "My favorite playground when we lived there."

Gathering all the cards to her, Claire laughed. "Do you remember the time my friend, Belinda, taught you guys to gig frogs?"

Liam's brows rose. "How could I forget?"

"What's frog gigging?" Veronica pursed her lips. "No. Don't tell me you killed frogs."

"Okay." Grayson's grin became lopsided. "We enjoyed it, though, we did it like hunting. We would spear bull frogs in the pond, cut off their hind legs, and Claire rolled the legs in flour and fried them." He licked his mouth. "Yum, good."

"Euw!" Veronica hid her face in her arm. "In my imagination, I can smell the pond on those legs."

"I made sure to skin and clean them good." Claire patted her sister-in-law's arm. "Honestly, they tasted better than chicken and were much more tender."

Liam held up a hand. "Okay, okay, let's not make her sick." He chuckled. "How about the time, Claire, when you made me mad and I left the cabin? Remember?"

She taped her chin. "Barely."

"You thought I went to the pond."

"Oh, I remember." She pointed at him. "You were a little squirt. Always sassing and making trouble."

"Well." He gave her a smug look. "I never went to the pond."

"What?" She twirled a curl around her finger. "Where did you go?"

He snorted. "Underneath the cabin. With Laddie. I heard every single thing you guys were saying."

Claire narrowed her eyes at him. "Oh." She waved a hand at Grayson. "And we thought you ran off to the pond, you little stink."

"I remember our dog, Laddie." Lolly raised a hand and wiggled it like she was in class. "Tell us something I'd remember."

Everyone grew quiet.

Claire opened her mouth, and then closed it. "I think, honey, you'd have to tell us a faint memory, and then we'd expand on it."

"Okay." Lolly bowed her head in what appeared deep thought. "I know." She stared at each of them, even Chipper, who of course didn't have any memories because he was a newborn. "I'm sorry you're left out, Chip, but maybe you enjoy hearing our stories?"

He waved her off with a rush of a breath. "I'm enjoying us being together, and I do like the stories. You guys are entertaining."

Lolly laid down her cards and clapped. "Okay. How about this one? We were sitting in front of a very tall lady who was scary looking. She had these black-rimmed glasses and really tall hair on top of her head. I know it's called a bun, of course. She kept asking you questions, Claire, and writing things down." Lolly tapped a fingernail on the table. "What I remember most was you were upset, Claire." She cast a questioning glance at her sister.

"The most vivid thing I recall is Grayson spoke to tell the tall lady something, and Claire shushed him with a hand over his mouth." Lolly laughed. "I wanted to giggle right there in my seat, with the way his eyes grew large and brows shot up." She shook her head, getting a fit of laugher. "Grayson, you looked like a snowball had smacked you in the face. But I didn't giggle. I was too scared." She touched Claire's arm. "Who was the lady, anyway? And why were we there and where were we, all four of us together?"

So Claire went into detail about their first day of school after Mama gave birth to Chipper in the cabin just hours before, and they both had to go the hospital. "The lady was the principal. And you had reason to be scared. I was scared too, but she made me angry, so my anger overrode my fear."

Chipper asked, "Why were you scared?"

"Becaaause," Claire drew out the word, "this principal was making Lolly go into Liam and Grayson's class. I knew Lolly would want me. I wanted her to be in my class so she wouldn't cry." Claire waved a hand as though swatting a fly. "But oh, no, I was only a kid and the principal was the boss. She felt she knew best."

Liam hollered. "Wrong!"

"Right." Claire nodded. "Lolly, you had a crying fit and could not be calmed." She pointed. "Liam came to tell me and my nice teacher allowed you to be in my class until Mom came back from the hospital."

Lolly nodded. "Ah, I see. I'm remembering more after you said all that. You gave me some crayons and I colored on green paper." She rested her chin in her upturned hand, smiling.

Dotty smiled also, feeling these stories may help her once-and-no-longer wayward daughter. This story surprised her, because no one had told her how they did on their first day of school.

# 10

After the last game of War, the girls broke away from cards and asked Dotty to play Scrabble. She jumped up from her recliner. Oh, yes. This was her favorite game. Even though she rarely won, it challenged her brain to make more than three letter words.

But when she checked the burl wall clock that Pete had made years ago, it was almost an hour past lunch. "Girls," Dotty raised a finger, "let's fix lunch first."

Her girls and Veronica followed her into the kitchen, and Claire sped ahead of her. "Mama, we have tons of leftovers. No need to cook. Just heat the food and set the table."

Lolly touched Dotty's sleeve. "Why don't you get the boys to move their game off the table and you could set it for lunch? We'll take care of the rest."

Moving to a cupboard, Dotty laughed. "Who's bossing who, now that my girls are mature adults?" Dotty sidled up to Veronica. "Sweetheart, I hope you don't think this family is too extreme."

Veronica, who stood a foot taller than Dotty, moved a strand of hair from Dotty's cheek. "Mama—" Her eyes grew wide as walnuts and just as dark. She bent at the waist to whisper, "Do you mind if I call you that?" She blinked.

In the background of the kitchen, Lolly and Claire giggled and snorted with laughter. Dotty pulled Veronica closer to the stove. "Honey, I'd be honored." Veronica's face blurred as her vision filled with moisture. "You may as well have been born to me, Veronica. I took to you the day Liam brought you home as his girlfriend those ten years ago."

Grabbing Dotty around the shoulders, Veronica sniffled. "I was hoping you felt that way. Mama."

She patted Veronica's back. "I do. I really do."

"I'll help you set the table." Veronica loaded her arm down with the paper plates and cups Dotty handed her.

Dotty followed Veronica into the dining room. "All right, you boys. Clear the table." Everyone of them jumped up and moved their cards.

"We're headed outside to see what Dad's doing, Mom." Chipper waved. "Holler when it's ready."

Dotty grabbed the flyswatter off its nail and swatted Chipper's shoulder as he headed outside. "Ow, Mama, I'm too old to be spanked." He lowered his chin and kissed her on the forehead. "Besides, I'm your best behaved kid. Admit it."

She swatted him again. "Yeah. Right."

He hollered, "Help me. Help me. My mama's beaten' me with a swatter."

Nobody paid him any attention as Dotty chuckled. She caught a whiff of honeysuckle from her porch and shut only the screen door. She hummed because her heart had grown happy.

\*\*\*

Lunch behind them, the boys went back outside to help Pete mend the fence where the skunk crawled through to get the chickens. Grayson offered to milk Jasmine so Dotty could be relieved of that job today.

Dotty and the girls settled down for their word game. Veronica had made a big pitcher of iced peach tea, and they were drinking it as they played. Having laid down a five letter word, Dotty clapped. "Would you looky there? Give me fifteen points." Knowing Lolly had taken her turn before her and they were both free to talk, Dotty had a burning question. "Lolly, where do you work these days?"

She blinked at Dotty. "I took some classes at the local college in childhood development and put out a resume. I'm a professional nanny."

Everyone gawked at Lolly. Then the questions began.

Claire moved her tiles around on her tile holder. "Who do you work for?"

"A husband and wife attorney team, the Souza's." A spark gleamed beneath Lolly's lashes. "I love the children, a boy and a girl, ages two and three."

Veronica had been leaning in, and Dotty could tell she had a question of her own. "Is it true you can live with the family when you're a nanny?"

Nodding, Lolly sifted through the tiny game dictionary. "Yes, and I do. I have my own room between the children's with adjoining doors so if they need me, I'll hear."

Claire's eyes grew as round as the cap on top of an acorn. "It's not that I don't believe you're good with children, Lolly. I just never thought of you as a nanny." Claire fingered a button on her shirt. "I'm impressed." She smiled.

Dotty had been waiting to ask something. "How long have you been in this nanny position, and did it come after the drinking and driving episode?"

Lolly's face pinked. "I'm still ashamed about all that mess. But after I became sober, my counselor helped me figure out my interests. What might be a good career." She bobbed her head. "I've worked for the Souza's for six months. Actually," she paused, "working with the children made me really miss my own family." She nodded again.

"So, I'm hoping this is a yes answer, Lolly." Veronica clasped her hands to her chest. "Please tell me you get to go on vacation with the family to some exotic island."

Laughing, Lolly set down the dictionary. "As a matter of fact."

The questions erupted.

"Where did you go?"

"Have you already been?"

"Tell us what it was like."

"I haven't gone yet." Lolly waved a hand. "But we're headed to the Azores in late summer. Both of the Souza's parents immigrated from two of the Azores Islands."

"I'm shocked." Dotty patted her heart. "The Azores are where your dad's people are from."

Lolly jerked her head from studying her tiles. "Are you serious? I never knew." She faced Claire. "Did you know that?"

"At some point, Mom told me." Claire shrugged. "Genealogy doesn't really interest me."

Settling against her chair, Lolly placed her hands on the table. "Maybe I can get more information about our family. Then I could ask the Souza's if we could take a day to visit where my family came from. That's if by chance it's close by where we're already going."

"I think we should get back to our game." Dotty leaned closer to Lolly. "But before we do, I wanted to tell you I'll ask your dad's aunt if she'll share her genealogy charts and notes with you."

"Super, Mama. Yes. Please do." Lolly picked up the dictionary again, a grin exposing her one dimple.

Veronica worked on her tiles, switching them around on her tile holder. "Whose turn is it?"

"Yours." The other three women shouted.

As the game continued, Dotty found out from the girls' conversation no one was leaving until tomorrow, Monday morning. She became so excited, she wanted to squeal like a little girl. Instead, she did what most mature ladies would do. She fought the tears within her lashes. "I'm thrilled."

\*\*\*

Pete and the four guys drove into town to pick up five large pizzas for supper. The women readied the table again, laughing, joking, and poking fun at one another. When Dotty's girls discovered Veronica hadn't eaten sugar in ten years, they pronounced her brave.

Lolly faced her and touched one of Veronica's thin shoulders. "Ever miss chocolate?"

"No. I bake treats using Stevia and honey." She shrugged. "I'm much healthier than before. Never worry about my weight, either."

"Ha!" Claire patted the small rolls on her tummy. "Wait until you have a few babies. Of course, I'll be getting huge again soon with the new baby." Her expression became dreamy as though she were already imagining her new baby in her arms.

Veronica's eyes froze. She lowered her chin and breathed in deep. "We can't have children." Her voice came out wobbly.

Dotty flopped into the closest chair, hands in her lap.

Claire's face shaded to a deep red.

Lolly hugged Veronica. "I'm sorry." Then she rested the side of her face on Veronica's shoulder.

Veronica sniffed. "Thank you. We're getting used to the idea, and we are filling out paperwork to adopt."

Both Claire and Dotty circled Veronica and Lolly. It became a group hug. No more words. Nothing even close came to Dotty for how sorrowful Liam and Veronica must feel.

Breaking the nurturing silence, all three of Claire's children ran from the toy room and barreled into the women. Tara said, "We want a hug too."

# 11

In the morning as the sun shone through the east kitchen window, everyone packed their belongings. Dotty made the coffee. For the tea drinkers, she put water on to boil. She sighed.

The time had come.

The children were leaving.

All would be quiet except Pete and Dotty's voices. The daily coo-coo of the mourning doves. The noises of the hens, with their contented cluck-clucks, their cackling spats, and hysterics over the laying of another fresh egg. Dotty couldn't forget her goats. They could be noisy, also. Her chest lightened at the farm noises which would keep her negative thoughts far away.

Was this considered counting your blessings?

Claire told her mom the night before to make an easy breakfast of oatmeal, because they would be in a hurry and not able to help clean up afterward. Donald had to get to work by ten o'clock. The cinnamon oatmeal with a dash of fresh-ground nutmeg had simmered three minutes. With the burner off, the mush finished cooking underneath a lid.

Cinnamon and nutmeg wafted through the air, making Dotty's stomach growl. As her family made several trips to their vehicles and back, she set the table with bowls and spoons. She placed a glass pitcher of goat milk on the table as well as a small pitcher of cream. A small bowl of brown sugar and one of raisins completed the oatmeal toppings.

If Dotty could make it so, this would be a fancy oatmeal breakfast, so she toasted a big platter of sprouted whole-wheat English muffins. Then, of course, she had to place butter, blackberry jam, and honey on the table.

She examined the breakfast spread and shrugged. Oops. She made a feast to please after all. Dotty never could make just one thing and not add to it.

As the last muffin popped up in the toaster, her girls peeked in. "Can we help with anything else?" Lolly asked.

Dotty gave Lolly the platter of muffins. "This is it."

With everyone seated, Pete gave the blessing. "Father, thank You for the hands who fixed our meal. Thank You that our family has this time together. Please give everyone safe travels. Bless this food to nourish our bodies. In Jesus' name. Amen."

Their last meal before they went their separate ways was filled with last minute questions about one another. Liam finished his oatmeal and pushed it aside. "Let's all work it out so we make this a yearly visit, alternating between Mother's Day and Father's Day."

Dotty and Pete glanced at each other, smiling.

Grayson stood. "Those who lack enough funds? We who can afford it will chip in so everyone will be here."

Chipper stood also, and grabbed Grayson by the neck. Head and shoulders taller than Grayson, Chipper gave him a knuckle scrub to the top of his head. "Yeah, because you're as poor as dirt, missionary brother."

Grayson's expression turned sheepish. "Well, yeah, I guess I'm poor. But, really, I was thinking of Lolly."

Lolly fingered the collar of her shirt. "That's mighty kind of you, Grayson."

And Dotty could tell Lolly meant it by the adoring look she gave him.

Claire got up from the table. "So next year, we'll meet here Father's Day weekend. Right?" She watched everyone's faces. They all nodded and agreed.

The goodbyes took half an hour, because it was hard for them to leave. But, after all, Dotty's children had lives of their own to live. Jobs to work. Children to raise. Homes to keep.

She and Pete waved and waved until the last vehicle disappeared out of sight.

And then.

And then. Dotty leaned into Pete's chest and broke down and cried.

\*\*\*

After feeding the goats and cleaning up the kitchen, Dotty started a load of wash. Pete came into the house, and they met in the dining room. He grabbed her hand. "Sweetheart, come with me." He led her outside, off the porch, and walked to the back of the property.

Was he going to show her the finished turkey pen? She was certain with the boys help, it was completed. But they passed the turkey pen. It was far from finished. Where was he taking her? The only building left in the direction they took was the barn. "Peter, what's this all about?"

He squeezed her hand. "Be patient, my love."

He was leading her at a fast walk, so she couldn't see his face. But she could hear the smile in his voice. "What are you up to, sir?"

"You'll see soon enough."

Yep. The barn. He was taking her to the barn. What could be so important inside the barn?

He stopped before the first step. "Close your eyes, Dot. Do not, and I mean, do not open them until I have you inside, and I tell you to look."

Dotty pursed her lips. "I'm going to trust you." But, of course, that went without saying.

Pete laughed. "Okay. Ready?"

"Ready."

His hand gripped hers as though she was his life support. She knew those steps by heart and did not stumble. Inside the cool barn, Dotty waited. She wanted to open her eyes. Instead, she kept them closed because she knew it would spoil his surprise.

"You can open them."

Dotty sucked in a breath. She took in the whole scene, not quite understanding. It wasn't her birthday, yet there were balloons. It wasn't their anniversary, yet there was a banner with the words, "I've loved you for almost forty years."

Dotty's jaw slackened.

Pete was holding her around the waist. His deep brown eyes were solemn. "Honey." His voice shook. He cleared his throat.

"Peter, is something wrong. Are you sick? Do you have bad—"

His finger on her lips stilled her words. "I'm fine. There's no bad news. I'm trying to tell you that I love you."

His face blurred.

He began again. "We started this journey just the two of us, so I wanted to bring your surprise weekend to a close with just the two of us." He fished inside his jacket pocket. "Here." He handed her an envelope.

Dotty took it with shaky fingers. "Oh, Pete." She opened it and gasped. There on the front page was a newly married couple in a two-seater convertible waving at a crowd of people as they drove away. The bride's veil flew behind her in the wind. The groom was at the wheel. On the back of the car it read, "Bride and Groom onto their honeymoon." Dotty turned the page. There was a living room scene with the married couple older. She was reading a book. He watched TV. Dotty read out loud, "We are still good together like peanut butter and jelly, a movie and popcorn, cheese and cracker. And the honeymoon will never end." Pete had written in the space below: "I've never been sorry I chose you. Yes, we've had harsh times. Yes, we've sorrowed over losses. Thank you for mothering our children, Sweetheart. Until death do us part is not just a phrase. I love you, Dotty Mariah Monteiro."

By the time Dotty read her name, the words were a shadowy jumble as her tears flowed. They hugged. Her voice gurgled. "I love you too, Sweetheart." Swaying in each other's arms, Pete reached out his hand. A sound like a flickering startled her. Dotty turned. An old projector played their wedding on a white sheet stretched on a barn wall. She was struck by silence. As the projector played, they were on their honeymoon in Florida. Then, Dotty appeared huge with pregnancy. Claire, a little baby in Dotty's arms. Then another baby, Liam. Clips of each of their children's births. All of them together after Gallagher Springs and back home in Oregon on their ninety-nine acres.

Dotty choked on sobs. Pete hugged her to him, murmuring soft words she could hear as there was no sound to the story of their lives. Then he squeezed her. "Lolly made this for us."

Her heart leaped. "I'm glad you told me. She's trying, isn't she?"

"Yes, love, she is."

They continued to watch as a newly married couple grew to a family of seven. The projector went blank. Pete switched it off. He led Dotty to a couple of folding chairs. He sat her down on the one with a soft throw pillow. "Wait here."

Dotty glanced around the barn. Pete had fixed the entryway of the barn party-perfect. He had pushed back equipment and tools where they sat in a jumble. Pete even swept the floor and, by golly, Dotty believed he even mopped. It appeared dust free. On closer inspection, the floorboards held a polished sheen.

Dotty got to wondering when he had time for this. She realized the turkey pen was not completed as it should have been with four strapping boys to help. Ah, so they helped Pete ready the barn.

Pete stood in front of her with two plates of food. "I made this late last night while you slept." He lowered her plate, and she accepted it.

Oh. Dotty couldn't believe it. She stared at him. "You did all this?"

His eyes gleamed, and he sat down beside her. "It was nothing."

"I beg to differ, sir, you made my favorite dish." Between two fingers, she pinched the California roll and bit into the delicious seaweed-wrapped avocado and rice. "Mmmm. Peter, this is the best." She popped the second half into her mouth.

"It's good then?" He shoved one in whole and chewed. With his mouth still full, he pointed. "When you're done with these, I have sweet and sour chicken on long toothpicks." He grinned when she opened her mouth. "I got your crock pot and simmered them on low all night long." He jabbed a finger to a little table she had not noticed before. "They're over there."

"Ahhh. So I wouldn't smell them cooking all night." She nodded. "Clever." Dotty ate the last of the three rolls, and then licked her lips. "How did you know to make these and where did you get the recipe?"

Pete's cheeks flushed. "I was hoping you wouldn't ask me that. I wanted you to think I created this idea all on my own."

"Oh?" She squinted. "Who helped you?"

He lowered his head and angled it to look at her. "Who do you think?"

"Claire, of course." Dotty giggled. "She has made them for me before."

Pete got up to serve them their chicken. He was only a few steps away. "Why don't you make this?"

She laughed out loud. "I didn't think you would like the California rolls and spicy chicken, being a bland meat and potatoes man."

He brought back their plates heaping with chicken, his piled twice as high and hers. "You think I like meat, huh?"

After they had eaten a few bites, she leaned closer and puckered her lips. "Sweet and sour kisses." Their lips met with a smack.

Pete wasn't finished. He leaned close to Dotty and deepened their kiss.

\*\*\*

Three days later, Dotty's wall phone rang. "Hello?"

"Dotty, uh, Mama?"

"Veronica, how are you, honey?"

"Ah," she sniffled, "we have news."

Dotty's heart froze in her chest. "What's wrong, baby? Are you okay? Is it Liam?"

"We're fine, honest." She sniffed again. "And you just said the word we're about to say."

"What?" Dotty frowned. Veronica wasn't making sense. It was obvious she was crying. But everyone's fine? "What—"

"Mama, Liam is here next to me, and we have an announcement." There was a pause. "We're having a baby!"

Dotty couldn't help herself. She screamed with joy. "Lord, have mercy!"

Liam's voice sounded loud on the phone. "Yes, He is merciful, Mama." He cleared his throat. "And Mama, are you sitting down?" No, she wasn't but she grabbed a chair and plopped. "We're having two babies."

Dotty covered her mouth with a hand. "What do you mean? Twins?"

Liam chuckled. "No, we've been approved to adopt a baby and we're going through with it. We're just not sure when we'll be receiving that little gift. This baby growing inside of Veronica will be born sometime around Christmas. Just like Claire's baby."

"Oh, Son. I'll call you back. I've got to tell your dad." Dotty hung up the phone and ran outside. She headed to the turkey pen and hollered, "Pete, Pete, you're not going to believe it."

Pete had a posthole digger and was taking dirt out of a hole. He let go of the digger and faced her. "What is it?"

When Dotty got to him, she flung herself into his arms. "We're going to have two more grandchildren."

# Author Biography

 Jean Ann Williams lives on the coast of Oregon with her husband Jim. She began her writing career in 1994 by reading a stack of books on the craft of writing. Since then, Jean Ann has published over 300 articles and short stories on the topics of Christianity, health, travel, friendship, relationships, family life, Sunday school take-home papers, and the loss of a child by suicide.

In her free time, Jean Ann enjoys Tunisian crocheting, reading inspirational books, gardening, and playing Scrabble with her grandchildren. Sometimes they let Nana win.

To learn more about Jean Ann Williams, visit her on her Facebook Author Page: https://www.facebook.com/Jean-Ann-Williams-848295125269670/Face Book and Twitter: https://twitter.com/JeanAnnWilliams.

# More books by Jean Ann Williams

### Just Claire

A mother damaged. The family tested. One daughter determined to find her place. ClaireLee must take charge of her siblings when her mother becomes depressed after a difficult childbirth. Claire becomes frightened because Mama sleeps often and has crying spells during waking hours. She finds comfort in the lies she tells herself and others to hide the truth about her erratic mother. Deciding she needs to re-invent herself, she sets out to impress the school's most popular girls.

### Road Trip of Delusion

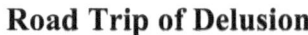

Fifteen-year-old Kari Rose discovers how much trouble she and her two sisters can get into when they stay at their ancient granny's for spring break. Granny gets a wild-haired notion at 3 a.m., and says she's leaving on a 500-mile road trip with or without them.

Kari takes her sisters and rides with Granny. Miles down the road, Granny is no longer able to drive, and Kari must take the wheel. The four travelers are caught in a snowstorm which brings everyone and everything to a standstill. Kari must determine the best way to find shelter and beat the storm. Will Kari trust her gut instincts and rely upon a complete stranger to lead them to safety?

### God's Mercies after Suicide:
### Blessings Woven through a Mother's Heart

What if your child shot himself while you were in the next room? What if you held him as his heart beat for the last time? What if Satan whispered in your ear, "Now where is your God?"

Find out how Jean Ann Williams reached out with her spirit and mind to the one true Father. Discover how the Lord God answered her and walked alongside her in the most difficult grieving journey of her life.

## Jean Ann's books are available on Amazon

*Sincerely Claire* a sequel to **Just Claire**~Releases Summer 2020
*Season of the Fawns* for New Adults~Releases Fall 2020

www.ingramcontent.com/pod-product-compliance
Lightning Source LLC
Chambersburg PA
CBHW030600130626
46552CB00006B/2607